TRIAL BY MAGIC
~ TALES FROM THE CASEBOOK OF THE WIZARD AT LAW ~

By Greg Fowlkes

Includes Sneak Previews from the Upcoming Books:

Star City Stories
and
The Fictional Detective Speaks with the Dead

TRIAL BY MAGIC

Published by Intrepid Ink, LLC

Intrepid Ink, LLC provides full publishing services to authors of fiction and non-fiction books, eBooks and websites. From editing to formatting, to publishing, to marketing, Intrepid Ink gets your creative works into the hands of the people who want to read them.

Find out more at www.IntrepidInk.com.

ISBN 13: 978-1-937022-70-9

Printed in the United States of America

BOOKS BY GREG FOWLKES

From the Wizard at Law Series:
The Laws of Magic
Trial by Magic

From the Murder on Mars Series:
Blood Red Sands of Mars
A Death at Station Alpha
A Corpse in Hut Town
Murder at the Mars Club

From the Fictional Detective Series:
The Fictional Detective
A Fictional Detective Trifecta

Star City Stories: A Collection of Stories Featuring Frank Sladek

The Uncorrupted Corpse

Tequila Visions

Cargo From Paradise

Ice Viking

FOREWORD

The world in which Egil Njalsson lives is very much like our own. It has Irish cops, good beer, shady property developers and crooked politicians. It has its own version of high technology which has brought consumers personal computers, e-mail and a host of other wonders practical and frivolous. One major difference between his world and ours is that magic is both real and practical, something that obeys laws that are as strict as those of Newton or Einstein in ours. Matter and energy can neither be created or destroyed, only changed in form according to rigid principles. It is a subject taught in the most prestigious universities and regulated by the full force of the law. And this is where Egil Njalsson comes in.

Egil Njalsson, whose exploits were first detailed in *The Laws of Magic*, is a young attorney with a small private practice. He also is a fully licensed wizard, having obtained his bachelor's degree from The California Institute of Thaumaturgy (the career change had seemed to make sense at the time.) As such, he is uniquely qualified to mediate in those cases where the laws of man and the laws of magic come into conflict.

The other important difference between Egil's world and ours is that all the creatures of legend and folklore in our world, such as demons, elves and ghosts or vampires, were-wolves, and zombies, are to be found walking down the street or living next door. They are also quite likely to walk in the door of Egil's office and ask for help with their legal problems.

The first of the stories in this volume. *The Ghost in the Machine*, involves an entrepreneur, who, finding himself dead, retains Egil's services from beyond the grave via the medium of e-mail to protect the inheritance of his niece and not coincidentally bring his murderer to justice.

A Wolf in Sheep's Clothing features a wolf with an unusual problem, he's been cursed by a native American shaman and must deal with the difficulties of being turned into a human during every full moon. And in *The Pot O' Gold* the client is a Leprechaun facing the loss of his saloon to the process of eminent domain.

Of course, not all of Egil's clients are supernatural in nature. In *What's this Zombie Doing in My Gumbo*, the client is a perfectly mortal chef who has been accused of turning a rival cook into a zombie. It should be noted that the zombie in this case is of the voodoo variety and not The Night of the Living Dead sort.

The final story, *Magic on Trial*, is something of a departure for the series. In it, Egil finds himself in court, not as council for the defense, but as a witness in a murder trial in which the defendant is accused of transmuting a man into a pillar of silicon through magic.

No matter how unusual the case, Egil does not have to deal with it alone, being mentored by a self described hedge wizard who seems to have as many personas as he does aliases. Jack Smith, or Jakob Schmitz, or whatever name he is using, may, or may not, be hundreds of years old, and may, or may, not have been a Tibetan monk, Lakota shaman, gypsy, rabbinical student, or any other of his numerous incarnations, but there is no question that he knows more about the obscure branches of the Art and Lore of magic than any living wizard has a right to. And of course, Joe O'Neil, Egil's friend the cop, is always ready to pitch in a hand when needed.

This, then, is a brief introduction to the world of Egil Njalsson, a world not too unlike our own, except . . .

Greg Fowlkes
GregFowlkes.com

ABOUT THE AUTHOR

Greg Fowlkes is a writer, musician and programmer. He obtained a Master's degree in Physics from the University of Wisconsin. Currently he lives outside of Madison, Wisconosin, with his partner Irene and two Shiba Inu dogs named respectively after a samurai actor (Toshiro) and one of that actor's more famous roles (Yojimbo). When not walking dogs, he enjoys reading, making craftsman furniture and playing the guitar and mandolin. His latest musical project is learning the playing style of gypsy jazz guitarist Django Reinhardt. Greg's series of books include The Murder on Mars series, The Wizard at Law series, and The Fictional Detective series.

TABLE OF CONTENTS

⋆ ⋆ ⋆ ⋆ ⋆

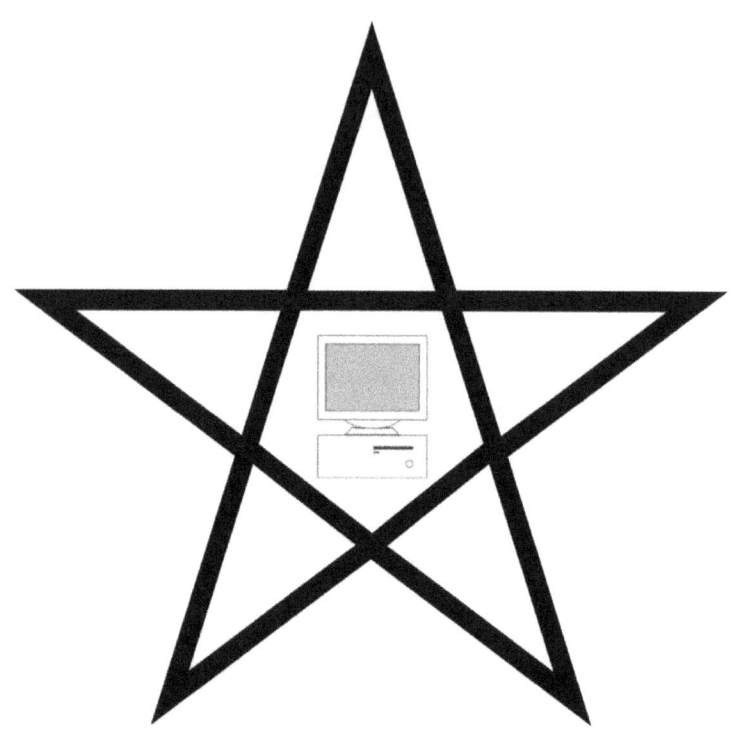

THE GHOST IN THE
MACHINE

THE GHOST IN THE MACHINE

☆ ☆ ☆ ☆ ☆

Egil Njalsson had never had a ghost as a client before. Vampires, werewolves, assorted other non-humans, maybe, but never a ghost. For one thing there was the question of how a ghost would handle his fees. For another, ghosts, as he understood the phenomenon, were usually restricted to a particular locality, which made it rather difficult for them to come to his office for consultations. Or make court appearances. That was what made the case so unusual.

It had started out innocently enough. His practice was finally doing well enough that he had been able to buy a computer. It was one of the new personal computers being marketed by International Divination Apparatus. His main motivation had been the fact that some courts were now allowing documents to be filed electronically. Not having to make trips down to the court house to hand documents over to the Clerk of Courts office could conceivably save him a lot of time. It came with word processing software and a billing package, not that his practice was so large that he really needed the latter.

Another bit of software was an e-mail program that would let him send and receive messages electronically. He didn't quite know how that worked. It seemed a bit like magic to him, though, of course, if it had been magic he probably would have been able to understand it. He had, after all, received a degree from the California Institute of

Thaumaturgy before going into the law. But, according to the manual that had come with the machine, e-mail involved converting a message into little bits of electricity and sending them down the wire to be reconstituted at the other end.

It seemed to Egil that there should be an easier way to do this. Perhaps invoking the Law of Similarity or some other form of sympathetic magic. But that would involve some fairly complex spells and require the sender to be a trained practitioner. Obviously, not everyone was skilled in magic. That was one of the great advantages of e-mail. Anyone with a suitable machine could send messages to anyone else with a machine all over ordinary wires with no magic involved. It did seem like a step backwards in that regard, but as with the telephone, which he also didn't really understand, the fact that it could be used by anyone seemed to insure that e-mail would soon be part of everyone's life.

After he had gotten the machine set up—and this had required a visit from a technician who's youth made Egil's thirty some odd years feel ancient—he had exchanged e-mails with a few acquaintances to make sure it worked. He had also received quite a few e-mails, mostly from people trying to sell him things he didn't want. He could see where that might prove to be a nuisance. He wondered if there was some sort of barrier spell that could be invoked to filter out such unwanted missives.

Along with the various e-mails, wanted and unwanted, had come one from what seemed to be a potential client. And this is where the ghost comes into the story.

The e-mail had seemed normal enough, an inquiry about retaining his services.

From: George Marsden
To: Egil Njalsson, Esq.

Dear Sir,
I am interested in retaining your services in a matter involving the probate of a will. If you are available, please contact me via e-mail at this address.

Yours,
George Marsden

From the formal phrasing it seemed that Mr. Marsden was as comfortable with e-mail as Egil was. However, the settling of wills was usually a simple matter that paid decently. While his practice had been doing better lately, it wasn't flourishing so well that he could afford to ignore a potential client. He responded:

From: Egil Njalsson
To: George Marsden

Dear Sir,
I would be glad to represent you in this matter. I look forward to meeting you. I would be happy to schedule a consultation at your convenience.

Yours,
Egil Njalsson, Esq.

To his surprise, there was an almost immediate reply:

From: George Marsden
To: Egil Njalsson, Esq.

Dear Sir,
Unfortunately, my circumstances make a face-to-face meeting impossible. However, I am quite prepared to discuss the particulars of the case via e-mail. I hope this will be acceptable to you. I am, of course, willing to pay all the usual fees. Are you willing to represent me in this matter?

Yours,
George Marsden

This struck Egil as somewhat unusual, but then the whole e-mail thing was new to him. He certainly had clients that he had dealt with mostly over the phone or through the mails. There was no reason, in principle, that e-mail might not serve the same purpose. He e-mailed:

From: Egil Njalsson
To: George Marsden

Dear Sir,
If conducting business via e-mail is most convenient for you then I see no problem with proceeding in that manner. I look forward to serving you. It is customary for an initial fee to be paid in advance as a retainer. $200 should serve for that purpose. Further expenses will be billed as incurred. Once I receive payment and the particulars of the case I will proceed as expeditiously as practical.

Yours,

Egil Njalsson

Again the reply was almost instantaneous, as if Marsden had been waiting for his e-mail.

From: George Marsden
To: Egil Njalsson, Esq.

Dear Sir,
I find your terms acceptable. I will arrange to have $1000 deposited to your account. Once the deposit has been made I will await your acknowledgment to forward the details.

Yours,
George Marsden

That ended the exchange of e-mails for the moment. For some reason, the name George Marsden seemed to trigger something in Egil's mind. At first he couldn't place it, then he remembered. He had seen it in the newspaper. He had a stack of papers for the last week in the corner. He found what he was looking for on the front page of Monday's business section.

Businessman Found Dead
Prominent software entrepreneur George Marsden was found dead at his office over the weekend. At this time the cause of death is still undetermined. Marsden was the inventor of the popular e-mail program "Mail Wizard" and was CEO of eWizard inc. Last January he sold controlling interest in the firm to a group of investors for a reported $350 million dollars, but retained a minority stake in the company and remained in his role as CEO.

When asked for a comment about the implications of Marsden's death for the future of the company, Harold Smith, chairman said, "While George Marsden's talents and insight will be deeply missed, his loss should have no effect on the company. He had assembled a very capable group of programmers and designers to carry on the tradition of innovation that has been a hallmark of eWizard."

Marsden never married, but is survived by a niece.

"What an idiot I am," Egil thought. The whole e-mail thing must be a hoax, either a joke or something to make him look foolish. Not that he could think of anyone who might perpetrate such a scheme. He didn't know much about the technical details of e-mail, but it must have taken quite a bit of effort to fake e-mail addresses. It was too bad, because he could have used the thousand dollars.

☆   ☆   ☆   ☆   ☆

Egil had all but forgotten about it by the time the next e-mail came in the following day.

From: George Marsden
To: Egil Njalsson

I am still awaiting your acknowledgement.

"Marsden" seemed to have gotten a little testy. He replied.

From: Egil Njalsson
To: George Marsden

Who is this? Is this some sort of a joke?

_____

From: George Marsden
To: Egil Njalsson

I assure you this is no joke. Please check your bank account.

One thing his new computer let him do was check the balances at his bank. He pulled up the information. Sure enough, there had been a deposit of $1000 to his business account from a George Marsden.

_____

From: Egil Njalsson
To: George Marsden

My apologies. I had assumed that you were the George Marsden who died this week—or rather that this was a joke by someone using that name.

_____

From: George Marsden
To: Egil Njalsson

I am that George Marsden.

_____

From: Egil Njalsson
To: George Marsden

The paper said that you were dead.

———————————————————————

From: George Marsden
To: Egil Njalsson

*That is correct. That is the personal circumstance
that prevents us from meeting face to face. I am in
fact dead. I am what is, for want of a better term, a
"ghost." I am still hoping that you will represent me.
I contacted you because you have a certain
reputation for matters that are, shall we say, "out of
the ordinary." I hope I have not misjudged you. I
need your help.*

Yours,
George Marsden

Egil wasn't sure how to respond. If he was indeed in
contact with George Marsden, deceased, which now
seemed at least a possibility, he wasn't sure where that put
him. He'd never dealt with a ghost before. Ghosts or spirits
were outside the scope of modern scientific magic. They
were not something that had been taught at CalThaum.
They hadn't been taught in law school, either. He wasn't
sure exactly what standing a ghost had under the law.

From: Egil Njalsson
To: George Marsden

Let's accept, for the moment, that you are dead and a ghost. I have taken a retainer to act on your behalf. Exactly what is it you want me to do for you?

_____

From: George Marsden
To: Egil Njalsson

Now you are starting to sound like the lawyer I had hoped you were. My concerns are twofold. One is that my wishes as expressed in my last will are carried out. I had modified my will so that my niece should inherit the bulk of my estate administered through a trust for all the usual tax reasons. I have reason to believe that someone will try to prevent this from happening. My niece is the only family that I have left. She is a sweet girl who I became very fond of in the last year. I wish to provide for her. The second concern is that I have reason to believe that I was murdered.

Now that was a bombshell. The paper hadn't mentioned anything about Marsden's death being a murder or even suspicious.

From: Egil Njalsson
To: George Marsden

You were murdered? Are you sure?

_____

From: George Marsden
To: Egil Njalsson

No. Oddly enough, I am not sure. It all happened so fast. One moment I was alive. The next dead. As you may imagine, being dead takes some getting used to. However, there is no reason that I should be dead. And, as you are aware, there is a great deal of money involved.

If I was murdered, I, of course, would like the culprit or culprits brought to justice. But, I want to make clear, my primary goal is to make sure that my niece is taken care of.

Egil thought for a moment about the best way to proceed. He would need to get more information than was in the papers, that was for sure. He would also need to research the subject of ghosts.

From: Egil Njalsson
To: George Marsden

Mr. Marsden, your case raises some interesting points of law that I will need to research. I will also need to make some inquiries into the facts surrounding your death. This may take a day or two. I will try to keep you informed. I hope that you will trust me to act in the best interests of you and your niece.

———————————————————————

From: George Marsden
To: Egil Njalsson

I am in your hands.

☆ ☆ ☆ ☆ ☆

Later that evening he was still sitting in his office when there was a knock.

"Mr. Njalsson?" came a woman's voice from the other side of the door.

He got up to open the door. There was a young woman, possibly nineteen or twenty, very attractive in a wholesome, co-ed sort of way. She looked as if she wasn't sure whether to be angry or embarrassed.

"I'm Egil Njalsson," he said. "Can I help you?"

"I want to know the meaning of this? Is this some sort of a joke, or are you just some kind of an ambulance chaser?" For the moment, the anger seemed to have won out. She thrust a piece of computer paper at him.

He looked it over. It was an e-mail. From Marsden to one Cynthia Harrow. It basically instructed her to contact him to act as her representative in regards to Marsden's will.

"I assume you are George Marsden's niece?" he asked.

"You should know that. Didn't you send me this e-mail?"

"No, I didn't. It would appear to have come from your uncle."

"Don't be ridiculous. My uncle is dead."

"Two days ago I would have said the same thing. However, in that time your uncle has been in contact with me through the medium of e-mails and has, at least provisionally retained me to act on his behalf."

"You expect me to believe that my uncle sent e-mails from beyond the grave?"

"The evidence would seem to indicate that. Now won't you please come in and take a seat so that we can discuss this in private?

The anger seemed to drain from her. She entered his office and took the chair across from his desk.

"Can I get you some water, a soda perhaps?"

"No, I'm fine," she replied, trying to pull herself together. "I just don't know what to think. My uncle's death was so unexpected."

"He said the same thing is his e-mail," Egil remarked.

"Is such a thing even possible?"

"It's an area in which very little research has been done. The subject of ghosts and spirits make serious researchers uneasy. It doesn't fit into any of the nice, neat academic categories of the Art. I think they feel it smacks just a little too much of crazy old ladies holding séances. But it would seem that your uncle is quite capable of sending e-mails, and of initiating funds transfers. He sent me a retainer from 'beyond the grave'."

"A retainer?"

"Yes. If it will put your mind at ease, I have already been paid for my services. I am not trying to con you out of any money."

"What then do you get out of this?" she asked.

"I will of course expect the customary fees for handling probating a will. I assure you my fees are quite reasonable, and as I've already received a retainer that should cover all the preliminaries, you needn't worry. Any additional expenses will come out of the estate once it is settled."

"Ok," Cynthia said. She didn't really sound convinced. "What do I have to do?"

"Well, the first thing is, I will need you to sign an agreement authorizing me to act in your behalf. While your Uncle is paying me, he doesn't actually have any standing under the law. I can only act for a living person. The agreement will allow me to file the necessary papers with the court. It will also mean that our relationship will be protected by the attorney-client privilege."

"Is that important?"

"I don't know. You're uncle seemed to think that the will might be contested, presumably by the same party or parties responsible for his death."

"Responsible for his death," she said. "Does that mean he was murdered?"

"Your uncle was uncertain on that point. He did seem to think that it was a distinct possibility."

"I see."

"Do you have a copy of the will?" Egil asked.

"No. I know my uncle mentioned that he had changed it, but I assumed it would be handled by his lawyers."

"That may or may not represent a problem. Can you give me the name of the firm?"

"Dewey, Cheatham, and Howe."

"I'll contact them and see if I can get a copy or make sure that you are present at the reading of the will."

"Is that it?"

"For the moment. I'll send the papers over tomorrow for you to sign. In the meantime, there is some research I need to do. Representing ghosts isn't something I do every day."

"Thank you, Mr. Njalsson," she said as she stood up.

"I'll keep you informed. And I'll let you know if I hear anything more from your uncle." He shook her hand and escorted her to the door of the office. He watched her walk down the hall to the elevator with more than casual interest.

He was serious about needing to do some research, but not the kind that could be done in a law book. He also felt the need for a drink.

He wasn't sure what Jack was drinking these days, but he wanted to keep a reasonably clear head. Fortunately it was early enough for the liquor stores to still be opened. He picked up a six pack of Munich Dark and drove over to Jack's place.

Jack Schmitz or "Old Jack" owned an antique store in one of the shadier parts of town. Not that he did much buying or selling. It mostly served as a front for his other business which was dealing in charms, potions, and the like. He also told the occasional fortune, read the cards, and for extra special customers he might even break out the crystal ball. Despite all the trappings, Jack was the real deal, a genuine mage, hedge wizard and shaman. He was never terribly specific about his background, and when he was, he never told the same story twice. If you believed half of the tales he had to be at least two hundred and fifty years old.

He had claimed at one time or another to be a druid, swami, rabbi, gypsy, brujo, and Tibetan monk. What Egil did know was that he spoke and wrote Hebrew, Roma, and at least a dozen Indian languages both American and Asian. He also had more practical knowledge of the Art than any five members of the faculty at CalThaum.

The store was closed, but a few moments after Egil rang the bell a wizened face peered out from around the shade. It broke into a smile and a second later the door opened.

"Egil, my son. It's been a while. I see you've brought gifts," he said nodding to the six pack. There was a slight Celtic lilt to his voice. Jack had been in Druid mode lately.

Of course his accent could change to match his current persona.

"What brings you to visit an old man?" Egil had represented him a few years earlier on a charge of practicing magic without a license. He had lost the case, but they had become friends.

"I felt the need of a drink," Egil answered. "I also want to pick your brain on something."

"Well come in. I'll be with you in a moment. You know the way."

Egil worked his way through the store to the room in back that served as Jack's study, living, and dining room. This was the sanctum that the customers never saw. The walls were lined with shelves full of books. Most of them were on the Art in a dozen languages, some quite old and rare. Several weren't even supposed to exist. There were also modern books on science and mathematics. The walls between the book cases were filled with old pictures of people in various costumes from around the world, a rabbinical class from around 1890 with a note in Czech, a picture of a Sioux medicine man in front of a teepee, a couple of Tibetan monks, and more that Egil had never had a chance to study. The curious thing was that in each of the pictures there was always a face that looked a lot like Jack's no matter what the race. He'd never figured out whether the photos were really of his friend or whether Jack just collected pictures that bore a chance resemblance to himself.

He rummaged around the kitchen area and came up with a pair of clean glasses. He believed that good beer should always be served in a glass. Bad beer just shouldn't be served.

"There's some sausage and cheese in the fridge. Help yourself. I'll be with you in just a minute," Jack hollered from the storefront. He found them and cut up some slices and threw them on a plate which he set on the table between the two Morris chairs in the center of the room. Opening two of the beers, he set the rest of the six pack in the refrigerator. He sat down in one of the chairs and poured the beers.

"So, what is this thing you want to ask about?"

"What do you know about ghosts?"

Jack took a sip of the beer closest to him. "This is good beer. You always did have good taste. So what do you want to know about ghosts? And why?"

"I've got one as a client."

If he had expected Jack to react he was mistaken. The old man took another sip of beer and then nibbled on a piece of the sausage.

"That's interesting. How did this spirit contact you? A Ouija board?"

"No, e-mail." This did cause a slight widening of the eyes.

"You never cease to surprise me, Egil. There's hope for you yet. What does this ghost want with you? An injunction against an exorcism?"

"No. He wants me to make sure that his will is handled properly. Also, he thinks he might have been murdered?"

"He thinks he might have been murdered? He's not sure? You would think he would know?"

"He said it took him by surprise. He wasn't expecting to die. I gather it was traumatic."

"Death usually is. But that would explain a lot. Ghosts usually only occur when there has been a violent, traumatic death. There is, in a sense, unfinished business that keeps the spirit from crossing over."

"Crossing over? To where?" Egil asked.

"No one knows. Once a spirit crosses over it never comes back. Maybe it just ceases to exist. Ten thousand years of religion hasn't come up with an answer, and anyone that claims to know is lying." Jack's views on religion were eclectic at best.

"So you think this ghost is hanging around waiting for some unfinished business to be taken care of?"

"That's the usual case. You say that the ghost wants to make sure his will is carried out?"

"Yes. He recently changed his will so that most of his estate goes to his niece?"

"You don't think she could have done it? The murder I mean?"

"No, she's a sweet young thing. I think it's more likely that the murderer is someone who would have benefitted from the previous will."

"Well, between seeing that his niece is taken care of and his murderer is brought to justice, there certainly is a strong motive for a spirit to remain. You say the ghost contacted you via e-mail."

"Yes. At first I thought it was just a normal client making an inquiry. He's contacted his niece by e-mail as well. Is that even possible?"

"Don't ask me. I don't know anything about e-mail. I don't even understand telephones. It's magic to me. Except if it was magic I might understand."

"You're being very helpful. Do you have any suggestions on how I should proceed?"

"Wills are lawyer business. Act like a lawyer. As to the murder, I think you need some evidence. That's a police sort of thing, but you may be able to give them a hand. If you find magic involved, then you can come to me."

"Great," Egil responded with a sigh.

"I'm sorry, Egil. I'd like to help you out, but I'm not sure there is much that I can do at the moment. If this Marsden is a ghost, then there is something keeping him here. It might just be anxiety over his niece, but it also may be a need for justice or vengeance. That would be the case if he was murdered. Why don't you see what you can find out. And let me know how things go. This ghost business is interesting."

"Thanks. Sorry for being so testy. It's just that I really would like to help this girl out. She's a nice kid."

Jack smiled, "Keep your mind on the problem, Egil. Don't get distracted by emotions."

☆   ☆   ☆   ☆   ☆

He finished up his beer and left. He knew Jack was right. If he was going to act on Cynthia's behalf he would need to get more information. Fortunately, by the time he left Jack's it was nearly eleven, time for a shift change for the police. If he was lucky he might be able to catch his one friend on the force at the diner next to the station. He usually stopped by for a bite to eat before heading home.

The diner wasn't much, some booths and a long counter. The food wasn't that great, either, but it was cheap and plentiful. The coffee was black and hot, and could keep a man awake during a long, late shift. The place was open 24 hours a day. Most of the patrons were policemen, particularly around shift change time. The back wall was covered with old pictures of men in blue uniforms, some so old that they had faded to brown.

He was a little early so he sat at the counter and ordered a reuben and coffee. He didn't have long to wait before a big beefy Irishman sat next to him.

"How's my favorite counselor?" the cop asked. Joseph O'Neil was one of the few honest cops on the force. He was also 6'2" and weighed 230 pounds. He had played football in high school and could take care of himself.

"Hi, Joe. Keeping out of trouble?" Egil answered.

"More than you are, unless I miss my guess?"

The waitress behind the counter put a cup in front of O'Neil and filled it with coffee without asking. "Usual?"

"Yeah, thanks Flo," O'Neil answered. The waitress guessed that we had something to talk over and left without making small talk.

"So what's up?"

"Do you know anything about the Marsden death?"

"Not much, though I was on the call. He was found dead in his desk chair by the cleaning crew. No visible signs of violence. I hear the medical examiner is going to call it 'natural causes' though he hasn't got a clue. Marsden's heart just stopped beating. Strange, he wasn't that old and looked like he was in good shape. I guess you just never know."

"Any chance it could be murder?"

O'Neil gave him the fish-eye. "You know something I don't, counselor? What's your interest?"

"I'm acting for Marsden's niece. Seems someone is going to inherit $350 million and I'm trying to make sure it's her."

"If it was murder, then no one has any idea how. There wasn't a struggle, no violence. The medical examiner did a real thorough job looking for poisons or magic. It's a pretty high profile case and he didn't want to be caught making a mistake."

Flo brought a plate of scrambled eggs over hash-browns with a couple of sausage patties on the side. O'Neil gave his attention to that for a couple of minutes. Egil ate his reuben.

"There is one thing, though," O'Neil said when he came up for air. "Like I said I saw the body before it had been moved. It wasn't slumped over like you might expect. It was almost like it had been thrown back in his chair. And the expression on his face. Jesus, I hope I don't see that again. It was a look of sheer terror. Maybe it was because he felt his heart stop, but I just don't know."

"Thanks, Joe. That's helpful." He threw a twenty on the counter and motioned to the waitress to take both orders out of it. "Keep the change." It didn't hurt to have Flo on his side.

* * * * * * * *

The next morning he devoted to leg work. He contacted the medical examiner's office about getting the medical examiner's report on Marsden. The person on the phone hemmed a bit, but when he told her that he was representing the next of kin and he would get a court order if necessary, she said that she would have a copy sent over by courier.

He waited until mid morning to call Marsden's law firm. He was a little surprised when the receptionist passed him right through to Walter Dewey, the senior partner.

"Good morning, Mr. Njalsson. I don't believe I've had the pleasure of working with you before," was the greeting in the slickest lawyer voice.

"I'm not usually involved in corporate work at this level," Egil responded in a tone that implied that he was absolutely not intimidated.

"Well, perhaps we can do something about that in the future," Dewey returned. "Ms. Harrow has informed us that you will be acting on her behalf. Is that correct."

"Yes, it is. I know the formal reading of the will won't take place for several weeks, but I was hoping that you could give me a head's up as to what we're looking at."

"Of course. I worked on the will, myself, George Marsden was a very important client of our firm. We handled both his personal and corporate work. I think the terms of the will were quite generous for Ms. Harrow. It establishes a trust to take care of all of her education expenses, and upon completion of her degree or her twenty fifth birthday pay to her a sum of one million dollars."

"I had thought that the estate was somewhat larger than that," Egil said.

"Oh, it is. Some of the money is to go to a charitable trust, the rest is to be split with Harold Smith and the rest of the original partners. I believe that all of the partners have such a clause in their wills. The intention was that in the event of the death of any one of the original partners, the others could carry on without having to worry about ownership being diluted. It's not that unusual in these high tech entrepreneurial companies. Of course the will was made out before George sold his holdings."

"Ms. Harrow was under the impression that there was a more recent will."

"Not that I'm aware of. This will was made three years ago, shortly after Ms. Harrow came to live with George. I thought it a very generous settlement at the time. Of course, eWizard wasn't nearly as big a company back then. This e-mail thing is really taking off. George may have been thinking of updating his will. It would have been natural under the circumstances, but as far as I know of he never acted upon it."

"Thank you, Mr. Dewey. You've been very helpful," Egil said in his smoothest voice. "I'm looking forward to meeting you in person at the reading of the will."

"Please, call me Walter. It's been nice talking to you. I hope that we can resolve matters to everybody's benefit. Good-bye."

The implication, of course, was that if he didn't make waves, Cynthia would receive a million dollars and he would have an in for some lucrative business in the future. All very nice. Unless there was a newer will.

There was one way to find out:

> *From: Egil Njalsson*
> *To: George Marsden*
>
> *I have just talked to Walter Dewey. He says the latest will is three years old and leaves your niece one million dollars. Is this the case?*

Marsden must have been waiting on the wire, or memory, or where ever ghosts hang out.

> *From: George Marsden*
> *To: Egil Njalsson*
>
> *He's lying. I worked with him, personally on the new will. It was signed, witnessed and notarized in his office. He is well aware of the terms.*

> ————————————————————————

> *From: Egil Njalsson*
> *To: George Marsden*

Who were the witnesses? Is there a copy of the will?

————————————————————————————

From: George Marsden
To: Egil Njalsson

The witnesses were Harold Smith and James Nyugen, my partners in eWizard. There was of course, a copy at Dewey's office. There is also one in my safe at home and in a safety deposit box at my bank. I also hid a copy in my office. No one should know about that. I had a secret safe installed. I don't think Smith or anyone else knew about it.

————————————————————————————

From: Egil Njalsson
To: George Marsden

I'll check your home safe and the box at the bank, first. Things are starting to look suspicious. Do you remember anything about your death?

————————————————————————————

From: George Marsden
To: Egil Njalsson

Not really. I was in my office. I was going to check my e-mail. The next thing I remember was that everything went black. It took me a while to realize that I was dead. It was not a pleasant experience.

————————————————————————————

From: Egil Njalsson
To: George Marsden

I think you were murdered when you accessed your e-mail. I don't know how. The police and the medical examiner haven't found any evidence of foul play. I think I may have to investigate this myself.

——————————————————————————

From: George Marsden
To: Egil Njalsson

I would appreciate that. My home safe is located in my study. The combination is 34L-22R-4L. Please take precautions so that nothing happens to Cynthia.

Shortly after the e-mail exchange ended, a messenger showed up with the medical examiner's report. It wasn't very helpful. The ruling was unknown 'natural causes.' There was nothing wrong with any of the internal organs. No sign of trauma. No poisons were detected. The medical examiner either had suspicions of his own or was being very careful to cover himself as he had ordered a lot more tests than is normal. Some of the poisons Egil had never even heard of, and he had taken some pretty good courses on the subject at CalThaum. The medical examiner had even brought in a professional witch smeller to detect signs of sorcery. That was highly unusual. No sorcery was detected, however. There were things that a professional might not detect, things that were so illegal as to not even be mentioned, but they weren't the kind of things they taught in universities. It was a good thing that he knew someone who didn't rely on his college education.

One thing was certain, he wanted to get his hands on a copy of the new will. If someone had killed Marsden, and that was still a big if, the changing of the will was probably the motivation. And if they had been able to murder him without leaving a trace that the M.E. could find, a simple office safe might not offer much security.

He phoned Cynthia Harrow and made arrangements to access the safe that evening. After he got off the phone he checked the contents of his "little black bag" to make sure that it had all the things he would require in case the safe was booby trapped. He also arranged to pick up Jack on the way over to Marsden's house.

Jack was waiting outside his shop when Egil drove up. He'd known the wizard long enough not to wonder about that. Jack had a way of knowing things. He also noted that Jack had his own bag of tricks in hand. It was considerably larger than his own. The old man put the bag in the back seat and climbed in next to Egil.

"Take a look at this," Egil said, handing him the medical examiner's report. Jack spent most of the drive reading it. Egil noted without surprise that he had no difficulty with the technical terminology.

"So we know what he didn't die of," Jack said when he had finished. "The M. E. seems to have been unusually thorough."

"Yeah, I noticed that. Any ideas?"

"There are many ways of taking a life. Some even I don't know."

Egil raised an eyebrow quizzically.

"I've never pretended that I know everything," Jack answered with the emphasis on the last word. "I just know more than they teach in your fancy schools."

"One thing I do know. I think you should be careful." The old man was dead serious. Egil always got nervous when Jack was concerned. He usually had a reason.

"That's why I asked you along," Egil said.

Marsden's house proved to be a large contemporary structure that was more glass than anything. It was set on what looked to be five wooded acres. From the back of the house a lawn area ran down to the shore of a lake. It looked like the kind of house a computer millionaire would own.

Cynthia was waiting at the door when they drove up. Egil wondered what it was like for her to be living in the place all alone now that her uncle was dead. As nice as the place was, he suspected it was cold and lonely.

Egil made the introductions. "This is Jack, a friend of mine. He's acting as a consultant. He's very good a spotting magic."

She looked a little uncertain at that, but smiled politely. She really was a nice girl, Egil thought.

She lead them through the house to Marsden's office and they got right to work. The office had a view of the lake with a big desk facing in that direction. A computer screen and keyboard sat on the desk, but the computer seemed to be buried inside one of the desk supports. No papers were visible on the desk top, just a lot of what Egil took to be teak.

The safe was set into a stone wall that also contained a large fireplace. A picture had hung over it, but that had been removed and set to the side. The picture was something abstract which mostly involved a large red circle. It looked like it was expensive. The safe itself was a top quality professional Swedish model. Egil guessed that you'd have to dismantle the wall to get it out. The shell was cold forged iron, proof against most forms of magic. Etched into the front and the locking mechanism were a number of runes forming a protective spell. Runes were unusual. Most wizards used Greek or Hebrew or Latin. It was probably due to the fact that it was of Swedish manufacture. Fortunately Egil was familiar with runic, and could read the spell. It was good work. Very professional. A safe like that probably cost twenty grand.

"Your client wasn't fooling around," Jack said as he examined the safe. "Not many burglars could handle something like this. Wonder what he intended to keep in it."

"My uncle used to bring a lot of work home," Cynthia responded. "Technical things. He was always concerned about security, afraid that someone might steal trade secrets. I gather from some of the things he said that industrial espionage was pretty intense in his business."

"Do you have the combination?" Jack asked.

"Marsden e-mailed it to me," Egil answered. He started to reach for the combination dial but Jack put his hand up.

"Let me check a few things first."

He opened his bag and began to pull out various bits of paraphernalia. Egil recognized most of it as the kind of stuff used to detect the presence of spells. A few of the items he didn't have a clue as to their purpose.

Jack spent about five minutes shaking rattles, drawing symbols on the front of the safe, dusting it with powders and so on while chanting in a half dozen languages that Egil recognized and a few he didn't. Cynthia looked on with curiosity. Laymen rarely get a chance to see real magic performed. When he was done he repacked his bag. and stood back.

"You might as well try to open it. If there is something magical inside, I can't detect it." He sounded a little uncertain, which for Jack was highly unusual.

Egil got the paper with the combination and dialed the numbers. After the last number there was the audible click of the locking bars retracting. He reached for the handle and gave it a turn. The door swung noiselessly open.

The inside of the safe was surprisingly large. To one side there was a stack of money. It looked to be about twenty thousand dollars in new hundred dollar bills. Several of the shelves had what appeared to be computer code and flow charts. Egil assumed that that was eWizard material. The bottom shelf had what looked like personal papers. Prominent was a large envelope on which was written "Will".

Egil pulled the envelope out of the safe and examined it. It was a normal, legal type envelope closed with a string. There was a wax seal holding the string closed. A notary's seal had been pressed into the wax. That was a typical spell to insure that the contents were secure. It wasn't a hard spell to break, but it was pretty hard to do without leaving a trace. This one was intact.

"With your permission?"

"Of course," Cynthia replied.

Egil took a silver knife from his bag and put it under the seal which popped free immediately. He then unwound the string from the fastening and opened the flap of the envelope. There was nothing inside.

"It's empty."

"May I see, lad?" Jack asked. Egil handed him the envelope.

Jack sniffed the seal, and examined the outside. He then looked inside. There was a shallow glass bowl sitting on a credenza against the far wall. He got this and placed it on the desk. He then took the envelope and upended it over the bowl. A small shower of pale dust fell from the envelope into the bowl.

"I think that is the will," Jack said.

"But how?"

"I don't know. The iron should have blocked any spell. So should the runes on the safe. I didn't detect any signs of sorcery. I'm baffled."

"You're saying there was a will, but it has been destroyed?" Cynthia asked.

"That's about the size of it."

"Maybe not quite," Jack interrupted. "I may be able to reconstitute the remains."

He dove back into his bag and brought out more gear. Most of it was unfamiliar to Egil.

"This is a trick I learned in Tibet," Jack said. He began to make passes over the bowl while chanting. Egil didn't recognize the language, but then he didn't speak Tibetan. It sounded as if Jack was singing two notes at once. It was pretty eerie.

A pale cloud began to appear over the bowl which took the form of a sheet of paper that glowed slightly and was semi transparent. Letters formed on the sheet. After a few minutes of chanting Egil was able to read them. He leaned over taking care not to touch the image.

It was a will, alright, dated a few days before Marsden's death. He was only able to read the first sheet, but the terms seemed to be what Marsden had claimed. Cynthia was to inherit the bulk of his estate including his remaining interest in eWizard.

As he straightened up Jack coughed.   The paper dissolved into dust once more.

"I'm sorry, I'm not as young as I used to be. There was a time when I could chant like that for twenty minutes straight."

"It doesn't matter. I read enough to know that that was the new will. The one that would give Cynthia almost everything. Unfortunately, I don't see that it does us any good. There is no way a court would accept that as a valid document. I'm sorry."

"I understand," Cynthia said. "You did your best. At least I still will inherit a million under the old will. That's a lot of money."

"Yes," Egil said. "The terms of the previous will should be proved by the court. But this makes it look more likely that your uncle was murdered. And as he is my client, I have a duty to bring the guilty to justice."

"I don't understand."

"If the will was intact when your uncle placed it in the safe, there is no way that it should have been vulnerable. That safe is top of the line, and the magics surrounding it were top grade, too.   Neither Jack or I were able to detect that they had failed.   That means that someone or something really good was involved. And I'd wager a million that they weren't using the approved arts to do it."

"The boys right, Miss Harrow," Jack said. "I've been around a long time and I don't miss much. I know something got to that will. I just don't know what or how."

"We can only hope that the other copy of the will is still intact."

"The other copy?" Cynthia asked.

"Your uncle said there was another copy of the will in a secret hiding place in his office at eWizard. We'll need to see if we can recover it before it is discovered."

"So there's still hope?"

"Yes, I think so. But don't mention anything about that to anyone."

"I understand, I think," Cynthia replied.

"Good. I think we should clean up here. I'll have to make plans to get access to your uncle's office. I'll let you know."

Jack gingerly poured the dust back into the envelope and restored the seal. It wouldn't fool an expert, but a casual look wouldn't detect that it had been disturbed. Egil placed it back in the safe and the closed the door.

When Egil dropped the old man off at his shop Jack bent over and said through the car door, "Be careful, lad. I don't know what we're up against, and that has me worried. It should worry you , too. Watch your back."

When Egil returned to his office there was a message on his answering machine from O'Neil. The cop said that he had something interesting to tell him and suggested they meet after his shift. It was still early enough that he could probably catch up with him at the diner.

O'Neil was sitting at the counter with a cup of coffee and a hamburger when Njalsson walked in. The cop nodded to the seat next to him.

"You've got something to tell me, Joe?"

"I picked up some dirt that I thought you might find interesting."

The waitress came over to take his order. The burger looked good so he ordered one with raw onions and fries on the side. After the waitress left he asked, "About the Marsden case?"

"Yeah. I got to talking to the detective who handled it. Seems that before it was ruled 'natural causes' he did some checking up on eWizard. Now when Marsden and his old partner sold the company they each retained twenty percent with the partnership that bought the company getting sixty. The partnership consists of three partners, each of whom ended up with twenty percent. You follow me so far?"

"Yeah. Everybody owned twenty percent."

"Until Marsden died. According to his will, Smith would get control of Marsden's share."

"Assuming that was the latest will that still wouldn't give Smith controlling interest."

"There's another will?" O'Neil asked with surprise.

"Maybe. I haven't found it yet. But get on with your story. Smith's got forty percent of the stock."

"Right, he's got forty percent. But the detective said that he'd gotten close to one of the investors. His share would give the two of them sixty percent and controlling interest. They'd pretty much be able to run the company the way they saw fit and in the end freeze out the other two investors. The word is they aren't terribly happy with the idea."

"That sounds like a motive for murder to me," Egil said.

"Yeah, that's what the detective thought until the M. E. couldn't find any sign of foul play." The policeman finished off his burger with one last bite. "So what's this about another will?"

"There's a rumor going round that Marsden had a new will that left everything to his niece."

"Interesting. Who'd you hear that from?"

"Marsden."

O'Neil looked over at the lawyer.

"Jesus. You aren't kidding, are you?" O'Neil had had enough experiences with Egil not to rule the possibility out. "You hold a séance or something?"

"No. He sent me an e-mail."

"I don't know whether to take you seriously or not. You want me to keep this under my hat?"

"For the time being. But if anything should happen to me, you just might drop a hint or two to that detective friend of yours."

"I'll keep that in mind. And you watch yourself, counselor. If you're right, Smith or his friend have already committed one murder."

"Believe me, Joe. I'm aware of that."

"Well I've got to be off or the missus will be upset." O'Neil got up and headed out. Egil noticed that he hadn't paid for his meal, but the information was certainly worth the price of a burger and coffee.

If the detective's information was right, and Egil saw no reason to doubt it, it certainly provided Smith with a motive. Control of a half billion dollar company would provide a temptation for most men. Now all he had to do was figure out how he had done it and how he was going to prove it.

Back at his office, Egil tried to figure out his next move. The most important thing was to secure the other copy of the will if possible. To do that, he needed to get in touch with Marsden.

From: Egil Njalsson
To: George Marsden

The copy of the will in your home safe was destroyed. I will need to obtain the one at your office.

————————————————————————

From: George Marsden
To: Egil Njalsson

Is Cynthia alright? What happened?

Egil noted that his client was more concerned with his niece than the will. It made him all the more determined to see the matter through.

From: Egil Njalsson
To: George Marsden

Cynthia is fine. When we opened the safe it appeared to be undisturbed, but the will inside had been burnt to ashes. We took all imaginable precautions, but I think it was destroyed before we got there. I don't know how. I had some expert help and he couldn't detect any tampering.

————————————————————————

From: George Marsden
To: Egil Njalsson

I don't understand. That safe was state of the art. It was solid cold forged iron and had the latest alarms both magical and electronic. It should have been completely tamper proof.

A flicker of an idea lit in the lawyer's mind.

From: Egil Njalsson
To: George Marsden

What form did the electronic alarm take?

_____

From: George Marsden
To: Egil Njalsson

There were sensors inside the safe. Any drastic change in pressure or temperature or excessive vibration and a signal would be sent to the security company.

_____

From: Egil Njalsson
To: George Marsden

Was there a wire that penetrated the shell of the safe?

_____

From: George Marsden
To: Egil Njalsson

Yes, there had to be to carry the signal. Do you think that that is how they got to the will? Is that even possible? To send a spell or something down a wire?

———————————————————————

From: Egil Njalsson
To: George Marsden

This from a ghost who's communicating via e-mail? All the signs are that whoever is behind this has access to some high quality professional wizardry, maybe even some demon help. The question is, does the safe in your office also have an electronic alarm?

———————————————————————

From: George Marsden
To: Egil Njalsson

No. I felt that the building security was enough. Besides, I kept the existence of the safe secret. Not even my partners knew about it.

———————————————————————

From: Egil Njalsson
To: George Marsden

Is there any way for me to get access you your office safe? Preferably without anyone finding out about it.

———————————————————————

From: George Marsden
To: Egil Njalsson

Unless they have changed the security system, I can give you a code that will open all the doors. I was always forgetting my key card, so I modified the security program so all I had to do was enter a code on the access pads. I don't think anyone knew. Harold and Jim always left details like that to me.

They exchanged a few more e-mails with the details of how to get into the office and open the safe. It was already 3 AM, too late to do anything until the following evening, so Egil headed home for bed.

Egil tried to get some sleep, but he found his thoughts kept returning to Cynthia Harrow, and not just as a client. He didn't meet many attractive women these days, they didn't usually need the services of a lawyer. The fact that she was attractive and potentially rich certainly had its appeal, but it was her courage and pluck that he admired as much as her physical attributes. He thought that she liked him as well. He'd have to work to keep things on a professional level, at least until the case was settled. It was nearly dawn before he finally fell asleep.

He arranged for Cynthia to meet him at his office that night around 10 PM. Once she arrived, he gathered his magic bag and they drove out to pick up Jack. As expected, he was waiting at the curb with his own bag of magical gear.

"It's been a while since I've done any breaking and entering, Laddy. You sure you've got this all planned out?" Jack asked as he slid into the back seat.

"Technically, we're not breaking in, just acting on behalf of a client who has every right to grant us access. I might take some persuasive arguing to convince a judge of that, seeing as he's a ghost, but I think the law should be the least of our worries. Marsden gave me pretty detailed instructions. If nothing has changed in the security setup we should be able to get in and out without anyone noticing."

The offices of eWizard were part of an office park on the north edge of the city. The main building where Marsden had his office was a three story rectangular building whose exterior was mostly glass and steel. Several similar buildings flanking it were used by the engineering and programming departments. The company had grown so fast in the last three years that they hadn't had time to develop a dedicated campus.

They parked away to the side of the programming building. There were a number of other cars parked there and lights on in parts of the building where people were working late. It was farther to walk, but Egil figured they wouldn't attract as much attention parking there.

There was a security station at the main entrance of the administration building with a guard behind the desk, but fortunately there was a private entrance along the side nearest where we had parked. Egil tried to look nonchalant as we walked along the sidewalk that ran in front of the buildings. Jack just seemed to blend in. He had a talent that way, like a chameleon. Once along the side they were out of the view of the guard.

The side entrance was set back into the wall, just a blank door with a handle. There was a 12 key keypad like on a phone set into the door frame and a slot for a key card.

I reached out to enter the number Marsden had given me, but Jack held up his hand.

"Wait a second."

He reached into his bag and pulled out a small pouch. Opening the pouch he reached in, pulled out a handful of dust and blew it into the air around Cynthia and Egil. Cynthia sneezed.

"Pixie dust," Jack explained. "It won't make us invisible, but it will make us less noticeable. It's an old poachers trick."

The entry code Marsden had given Egil seemed to work. There was a loud click, and when he pulled on the handle the door edged open. He looked around, but no one seemed to have noticed.

The door opened into a long corridor. Overhead lights every fifty feet or so provided a dim illumination. There didn't seem to be anyone around. Three doors down the hall there was another door with a keypad and card reader. This opened into a stairwell. Marsden's office was on the top floor in the northeast corner. The same code worked for this door, too, and the three of them entered and went up the steps.

At the top landing, Egil stopped them and pressed his ear against the door into the hallway. Off in the distance he could hear a faint humming sound, but nothing in the corridor on the other side of the door. A code wasn't needed to exit the stairwell. Egil turned the handle, edged the door open and looked around. The corridor was clear.

There was another keypad and card reader on Marsden's office suite. The company had taken security seriously even if Marsden hadn't. There was an outer office and waiting room for his secretary with Marsden's office beyond that. There was no security lock on that door.

Two walls of the office were glass with no blinds or drapes. Fortunately, there was enough light coming in from the parking lot that they wouldn't need to turn on the overhead lights. The other two walls were wood paneling with the usual pictures and awards hanging on the wall. The office furniture was all chrome, walnut, and leather with a desk, a conference table, and a seating group. The office was bigger than Egil's apartment. Marsden's desk was against one of the paneled walls looking out to the north. It looked like a nice view with some trees and wetlands behind them.

Set low against the wall behind the desk was what looked like a ventilation grill. Egil pressed the four screws in the corners of the grill in the order Marsden had given him. There was a pop as a catch released and the grill swung aside. Inside, behind the grill was another Swedish safe, smaller than the one at Marsden's home.

Jack went through the same routine he had used at Marsden's home. When he was done, he shrugged his shoulders. "It's all yours."

Egil dialed the combination and the door came open. There were a number of papers, but sitting on the top shelf was an envelope identical to the one they had found at Marsden's house.

Egil reached for it and laid it on the desk.

"Do you think we should open it?" Egil asked, looking at Jack.

"I don't sense any magic. Might as well get it over with."

Egil slit the seal with his silver knife. He could feel the thickness of several sheets of paper inside. Gingerly he opened the flap and extracted the papers. He examined the first page with a small flashlight. It was the will.

Suddenly the lights went on.

"I'll take that," came a voice from the doorway. A man was standing there, a automatic pistol gripped in his hand. Egil recognized him as Harold Smith, Marsden's former partner. "And please don't move. I want the three of you where I can keep an eye on you."

The three of them had gathered together to look over the will, presenting a convenient target for Smith.

"I'm afraid I can't hand this over to you," Egil found himself saying. "This is the property of my client." He looked at Jack out of the corner of his eye hoping that the older man had some trick up his sleeve. The helpless expression on his face offered no reassurance.

"I don't think you are in any position to argue, Mr. Njalsson. I am the one holding the gun. And after all, you are the one who broke in. You and your friend do have something of a reputation as powerful wizards. I think I could make a credible case for self defense if I shot you, and if Ms. Harrow were to be killed in the exchange, well that would just be regrettable collateral damage."

"I will point out that we did not 'break in' as you put it, but used a valid password supplied by one of the officers of this company."

"And who might that be?" Smith asked snidely.

"George Marsden, who I believe has not yet been replaced as CEO."

"Come now. Njalsson. Marsden is dead. He died in this very office."

"A mere technicality. I don't believe that the board of directors has seen fit to name a replacement as of yet."

"The board has merely been waiting for the status of Marsden's shares to be decided before holding a vote. But this is all nonsense. As I said earlier, I'm the one holding the gun."

"And you've already committed one murder, haven't you?" Egil stated.

"Yes, I did, but no one will ever be able to prove it."

"Exactly how did you manage it, Smith? I have to admit that it must have been a pretty clever piece of work to avoid detection. Who did you get to supply the spell?" Egil was trying to buy time. He wasn't sure for what, but they didn't seem to have any other option at the moment. Now that Smith had admitted to killing Marsden, it was unlikely that he would let them live.

"You're just like the others. Everyone always thought Marsden was the only technical genius in the firm. That I only handled the business side of things. But I've done my share of the work, even though I never got the credit for it."

"I think I will tell you how I did it, Njalsson, not that you'll ever be able to tell anyone else."

"You know that the secret behind eWizard is the interface between computers in this world and the 'ether' in the other world. That's how e-mails get from one machine to the other, they don't travel in this world, but, through the application of magic, pass through the other world to reach their destination. That's why it's called the 'ethernet'."

"As a wizard, Njalsson, you must know that the spirit world is a pretty strange place. We had to do a lot of work to create firewalls to keep unwanted forces from penetrating through to this world using the computer interface. That was my job, my part of the eWizard solution."

"Well, I learned a lot about the other side. And I learned how to control those forces and send them through wires. You saw an example of that with the safe at Marsden's house. I sent one of the entities from the other side along the sensor wire to destroy the will. You have to admit that was pretty clever, don't you, Njalsson?"

"It sounds like you've been consorting with demons, to me. That's a dangerous business."

"Demons, maybe. It's all a matter of semantics. The important thing is that I control them."

Jack spoke up for the first time, "One never controls a demon. At best one can restrain them. Only a fool would open a gateway to the other world for demons to use."

"Njalsson, really. From what I've heard your old hedge wizard here has had plenty to do with the black powers."

"Only to keep them from this world!" Jack exclaimed.

"I've had enough of this talk, If you have any last words you want to say to each other, I suggest you say them now." The gun in Smith's hand was looking bigger than ever.

At that moment, the screen on Marsden's desk came to life and emitted a loud beep.

"What's your game, Njalsson?"

"I didn't do anything. I thought the computer was off. But there seems to be an e-mail. It's for you."

"What kind of a fool do you think I am?"

"Look for yourself."

Smith's curiosity got the better of him. "Back away from the desk, and don't try anything. Remember, the girl get's it first."

They moved into the corner to let Smith come around the desk.

The screen was displaying the following message.

From: George Marsden
To: Harold Smith

Harold, why did you do it? Weren't you rich enough?

Following that was a transcription of the conversation from the time Smith had entered turned on the lights.

"George, you always were too naive. I think I'll just delete this."

Smith reached over with his left hand to hit the delete key. As his finger touched the keyboard there was a crackle of light. Smith slumped to the desk, the gun dropping from his hand.

Egil reached over to check Smith. Jack grabbed the gun.

"He's dead. My guess is that the medical examiner will find the same lack of causes as he did with Marsden. We'd better call the police."

Just then the computer beeped once more. A new e-mail appeared on the screen.

> *From: George Marsden*
> *To: Egil Njalsson*
>
> *I want to thank you for your services in this business, Mr. Njalsson. They exceeded my expectation. I have forwarded payment to your account. This will be the last communication between us.*
>
> *Good-bye*

The message stayed on the screen for a few moments, then the computer went dark.

Smith's death was ruled as due to "natural causes," the same as Marsden's. The will from Marsden's office was ruled valid. Cynthia Harrow ended up a very wealthy young lady. True to his word, Marsden had transferred a payment to Egil's account. It was very generous. He wouldn't have to worry about rent or groceries for a long, long time.

A couple of months after the will went through probate Cynthia stopped by his office to thank him for everything.

She had a young man in tow. They were getting married in the spring. He was invited to the wedding. He wished the couple the best of luck.

He had tried to contact Marsden several times via e-mail. Every time he did, the e-mail was rejected with the message:

Address Unknown

A WOLF IN SHEEP'S CLOTHING

A Wolf in Sheep's Clothing

☆   ☆   ☆   ☆   ☆

The dark clouds scudded across the sky, occasionally parting to reveal the bright orb of the full moon. The wolf's ears pricked as he ran through the woods. The deer, a fat buck, was running ahead of him, crashing through the underbrush. The buck was wounded and there was the scent of blood in the crisp night air.

There was another sound, too, and a smell. Man! The wolf wasn't the only hunter that night. The man was after the deer, as well. But the wolf wasn't afraid, and he was hungry, too.

The deer was closer. The wolf quickened his pace, running faster than the man. He would get to the prey first. Suddenly the deer stopped, exhausted, bleeding, and turned to face the wolf in one last stand. A leap, fangs closing on the throat, the deer down, struggling and then lying still.

The wolf had just begun to feed when the man came up. He turned, fangs bared, a snarl rising from his chest.

"Damn wolf," the Man said. He was big for a human, and still strong despite his age. And there was a smell of power about him that the wolf knew was not natural. But there was another smell about him, too, a sweet smell the wolf couldn't place.

"Thas my deer, Mr. Wolfie," the man said, his words slurred by alcohol. The wolf snarled in response.

"Back off, Wolf. You don't know what your messing with." The wolf crouched, readying himself for a lunge at the man. But the man wasn't afraid. He straightened up, somehow seeming even taller, taller than a Man had any right to be. There was fire in his eyes, and the man began to chant. As if on cue, the clouds parted and the wolf found himself caught in a beam of moonlight.

When the wolf awoke he was cold, shivering. That was odd as the night had not been cold. He felt strange, confused. He sniffed the night air, but his nose didn't seem to be working right. He tried to stand, but his muscles didn't respond the way they should. He looked at his paw, but it wasn't a paw. It was a man's hand. Struggling to get his legs under him, the man who had been a wolf sat on his haunches and howled at the full moon.

☆   ☆   ☆   ☆   ☆

It was a full moon. Egil disliked full moons. You never knew what might come out, and Egil, more than most, had a good idea of the possibilities. Though currently a lawyer with a small but improving practice, he had done his undergraduate work at the California Institute of Thaumaturgy, the best school of magic in the country. He was only too aware of the various and often dangerous beings that could cross over from the half world on nights when the moon was full. Not to mention the effects the lunar orb had on many of the denizens of this world. The term "lunatic" was firmly grounded in scientific reality.

That was why Egil took note when the hairs on the back of his hand stood at attention. He sniffed the air intently. It's a little known fact among laymen that many supranatural phenomenon produce distinctive odors detectable to a trained nose. Egil was by no means a "witch finder," but he had enough training and experience to detect the most obvious threats, and he didn't like what he was sensing. It was similar, but not identical to, the taint of a werewolf. He sat up straight in his desk chair looking expectantly at the frosted glass panel set in his office door.

A moment later the shadow of a human form appeared silhouetted by the hall light. A hand reached up and knocked on the door frame.

"Hello, is anyone here? I'm looking for Egil Njalsson, the lawyer."

"Come in," Egil said, somewhat reluctantly. If he had been expecting a vampire he would not have offered the invitation, but with a werewolf the old restriction against entering uninvited was powerless.

The door opened and a young man entered tentatively. He was small, barely five feet and didn't look to weigh more than a hundred pounds. He had eyes of an extraordinary piercing pale blue. He might easily have been taken for a boy, but there was a wiry strength about his lean, sinewy body that indicated he might be a dangerous foe if pushed. There was also no doubt that the "were" emanation was arising from him.

"Are you Egil Njalsson, the lawyer?" the young man asked.

"I am. What can I do for you?" Egil asked carefully.

"I'm in need of some legal help, and I've heard that you have experience with cases that are, shall we say, out of the norm."

Egil wondered, not for the first time, if having his reputation was a good thing. It certainly had brought him a number of clients who paid well, but not without risk.

"Have a seat. What exactly can I do for you Mr. —?"

"Thank you," the client said seating himself but not offering his name.

"Excuse me, but you are a werewolf, aren't you?"

"Not exactly."

"What exactly are you? If I am going to take you on as a client, I will need to know what I'm dealing with."

"I'm, for want of a better term, a were-human."

"A were-human?" Egil asked with surprise. He had thought he was up on the lore, but this was a new one for him.

"The fact is, that I am not a human. I am a wolf that turns into a man every full moon."

Egil had never heard of such a thing, but for the moment he decided to suspend his disbelief. His nose, at least, seemed to indicate that there was something unusual about the slight man that sat in the chair opposite him.

"If you don't mind my asking, how exactly did your condition come about?"

The were-man sighed. "It was a curse. A Native American shaman, Ojibawa I think. He was drunk. We had been hunting the same deer during a full moon. I got there first. He cursed me. I turned into a man. And every full moon since I turn into a man for a period three to five days."

"Do you mind my asking, if you are a wolf, how you come to speak English so well?"

"I can't tell you. All I know is that when I am in the form of a man I have all the knowledge you would expect a man to have. I can speak English, I can read, I even speak Ojibawa. When I return to being a wolf, I lose those abilities."

"And the shaman? Have you approached him about undoing the curse?"

"He died. He drowned when his canoe overturned that same night. As I said, he was drunk. I've approached others about my plight, but no one seems to have any knowledge of such a curse or how to undo it. As you can imagine, the transformation is inconvenient and unpleasant. I don't want to be a man. I was quite happy being a wolf. Being a man is so complicated."

"I might know someone who could help. I'll mention it to him. But I take it you came to me about a legal problem and not your curse."

"Yes. If I am going to keep turning into a man, I need someplace to stay. Someplace I can store clothing and other things I need as a man. There's a small plot of woodlands with a cabin that I would like to purchase. I have some money coming to me, but as a wolf, there's no way that I can complete the transaction."

"I see," Egil said. He wasn't sure he wanted to know how a wolf came by enough money to buy a cabin, but as a lawyer he knew enough not to ask questions that he didn't want to hear the answers to.

"I'll have to do some research, but I might be able to arrange a trust of some sort that would be legally empowered to own the property, pay taxes and handle any other financial matters that might arise. I can set things up so that I have power to conduct any necessary transactions."

"That sounds like it would be acceptable,"

Egil thought that for a wolf, his client seemed particularly well organized and businesslike. Egil got the particulars of the property, who the current owner was, and the sale price.

"It will take me a few days to arrange the paperwork. I don't suppose there is any way for me to contact you?"

"Not for the next month. But if you will get the paperwork together, I will call on you in four weeks time."

"That should be ok. I will arrange to be here. Is there anything else?"

"No. I'll be on my way." The were-man rose abruptly and went to the door.

"Just for convenience, what should I call you?"

The were-man paused in the doorway and thought for a moment, then said, "You can call me Wolfe, John Q. Wolfe." He smiled, revealing a set of very prominent set of teeth, and then left.

Now this wasn't the first time something strange had walked into Egil's office. In fact, it seemed to happen with disconcerting regularity. But the concept of a were-human was a new one to him; something beyond his experience and training. Before he proceeded, he felt the need for some expert advice, and experts never came free. He opened the lower drawer of his desk and withdrew an unopened bottle of Irish whisky.

☆ ☆ ☆ ☆ ☆

The sign on the run-down shop said antiques, but Egil knew better. Most of the contents of the shop were just junk, and Egil doubted if the proprietor ever sold any of it. Mostly, it just served as window dressing, providing a cover for the real business that went on in the back room.

Finding the front door unlocked, Egil entered. A tiny bell over the door tinkled as it shut behind him, and a voice from the back cried out, "I'll be with you in a minute."

"Don't rush, it's only me," the lawyer responded.

A few minutes later the proprietor of the store came out of the back room escorting a middle-aged woman dressed in a prim black dress, the sort of thing she might wear to a funeral.

Turning to face the old man at her elbow, she said, "Thank you, again, Mr. Smith. I always feel so much better after our sessions. Same time next month?"

"That will be fine, Mrs. Benjamin. I'm always glad to be of help. Just remember what I told you, you must be on guard against charlatans that want to take your money."

"Oh, I will, Mr. Smith. Don't you worry about that." After taking a long, hard look at Njalsson, she left through the front door.

The old man waved, and then turning to the lawyer said, "Oh, don't give me your disapproving look. There's no harm in what I do. For ten dollars once a month, I give her tea and biscuits and tell her what she wants to hear. So I read the cards and maybe gaze into a crystal ball. It's all harmless entertainment, and it keeps her from doing anything foolish. You know there are people out there who would love to separate a widow from her money."

"I'm sure," Egil said with a chuckle. It was true that Old Jack, or Jakob Schmidts, or whatever name the old man was using that month did a small trade in telling fortunes and providing potions and protective charms, but he always operated in what he, at least, considered an ethical manner. And the charms, unlike many, were the real deal.

"So what brings my favorite counselor to this humble abode? What sort of trouble have you gotten yourself into this time?"

"No trouble. It's just that I've taken on an unusual client and I'm looking for some background information."

"Sounds intriguing. Why don't we retire to the inner sanctum. I trust you've brought a little something to lubricate the brain cells."

Egil brought out the fifth of whisky from his coat pocket and handed it to the old man.

"You're a good lad, Egil. Not many respect their elders the way they should," he said as he parted the curtain that hung on the doorway to the back room.

If the front room was a jumble; the backroom was, in complete contrast, neat as a pin. Two walls were covered with a rank of bookcases filled with a miscellany of volumes, while another held a collection of old photographs. The books, which Egil knew from previous examinations, ranged in age from a few years to a dozen centuries and constituted one of the best libraries of magical works in the country.

In the middle of the room was a simple table covered with a black cloth and with two chairs facing each other. In the middle of the table was an object about eight inches high covered by a velvet cover. Egil knew that underneath the cover was a crystal ball. A deck of Tarot cards sat neatly to the side. There was also a tea pot, two cups, and a small plate of cookies.

"Give me just a minute to clean up," Jack said, setting down the whisky bottle and picking up the tea pot. "Make yourself at home." He retreated up a narrow staircase at the back of the room to the kitchen above. A moment later he returned with two crystal tumblers. With a flourish he opened the bottle and poured three fingers of the amber liquid into each glass.

He pushed one of the glasses over to Egil. "Slange," he said sipping from his own tumbler.

Egil's friend had taken on the persona of an Irish gypsy horse-trader this month, the last of a long line of travelers occupied in that trade. Of course, the previous month he had claimed to be an Indian swami, and the month before that a Tibetan monk. The month before, he couldn't remember. Whatever the story, he maintained the fiction flawlessly, changing his accent and mannerisms to match. Egil wondered what his customers thought of the changes, but he suspected they thought he was just channeling different spirits.

Of course, looking at the wall of photos, he remembered seeing one of a gypsy caravan from the late 1800's. The man holding the reins of the horses bore more than a passing resemblance to the man sitting across the table from him. The picture next to that was a group photo of some rabbis in Vienna back before the breakup of the Austro-Hungarian Empire. The third rabbi from the left, if one allowed for the beard and side curls, looked a lot like Jack. There was also one of a group of Indians and Army officers taken at the signing of a peace treaty. Jack's face stared out from underneath the buffalo headdress of an Comanche shaman standing in the back row. Egil never had been able to get a straight or consistent answer about Jack's origins. He was certain that the man was older than he looked, which was saying something, but just how much older was an open question.

"So, tell me about this client."

"Have you ever heard of a were-human? I don't mean a were-wolf or anything like that, I mean an animal that gets turned into a man every full moon."

"That's a good one, Egil. You really know how to think them up."

"I'm serious. Is it possible?"

"Tell me what this man looked like?" Jack said, suddenly at attention.

"He was thin, maybe a hundred pounds or so. Lean and muscular. The backs of his hands were quite hairy as was his neck. His ears had a hint of a point to them. He had pale blue eyes."

"That certainly sounds like the real thing. The hair and the pointy ears you might expect from the wolf nature. The weight makes sense, too. After all, a full grown wolf doesn't weigh nearly as much as a man. Mass would have to be conserved in any transformation. Let me think a bit."

Jack took a distracted sip of whisky. "I seem to remember reading something once. Now where was it." He got up and started to look over the volumes in his bookshelf. "Ah, yes, I think this is it," as he pulled out a slim leather bound volume that looked as if it could be three or four hundred years old. "Lucian of Parma," he said. "It's in Latin, but the title translates to something like 'Strange Occurances.' There's a case he reports of in Dalmatia, about 450 A. D. or so. Of course Lucian was writing several centuries later, but he was using some old church records."

He thumbed through the book until he came to the passage he was interested in. "I won't translate the whole thing. Basically, it's a report of a naked man being found by a bunch of villagers. He acted crazy and he didn't seem to understand any language. They locked him up in a room of the church while they decided what to do with him. The priest who wrote the original account said that this happened during the full of the moon and that he thought the man might be a lunatic. Anyway, they kept him locked up for a few days. But on the third day, when they went to take him some food and water, they found the man gone and a wolf in his place. The wolf got loose and ran away. But for several months after that, during the full moon, the villagers reported seeing a naked man running on all fours and howling pitifully. Meanwhile, a wolf had been plaguing the villagers, attacking sheep and such. They finally cornered the wolf and killed it. After that there were no more appearances of the naked man."

"So you think the man was actually the wolf?"

"Could be. Lucian is kind of vague on that. He's just recounting the story. But he does say that at about the same time, there was a powerful sorcerer operating in the neighborhood. He speculates that perhaps this sorcerer cast a spell on the wolf just to cause trouble. How does your man-wolf explain his condition? I take it he does talk?"

"Actually, he spoke quite well, and seemed quite rational. He claimed that a drunken Native American shaman put a curse on him one night when they were hunting the same deer. The shaman drowned the same night when he fell out of his canoe, thus he can't undo the curse. This happened up in the northern part of the state."

"I see. I've heard of a powerful shaman operating up there, though I've never crossed paths with him. From rumors, he might have been strong enough to pull something like this off."

"I don't suppose there is any way to remove the curse? My client would rather remain a wolf full time."

"Very sensible of him," Jack commented. "I'm afraid this is kind of beyond me. A curse like that is very dark magic indeed. Without knowing the specifics it would be nearly impossible to counter act it. I'm afraid your client will just have to live with it."

"He seems resigned to that possibility. He actually seemed very intelligent and civilized. For a wolf."

"Just what did he want you to do for him? If you don't mind my asking."

"If he's going to keep turning into a man, he wants to buy a cabin where he can hole up during the full moon. A place where he can keep his clothes during the part of the month when he's not a man."

"Sounds sensible. Do you think you can do it?"

"He says he has enough money to buy the place. I'm not sure how a wolf could come up with that kind of cash. The problem is, how do I put it in his name? I'm thinking of setting up some kind of trust with me as the administrator. That way I could take care of the taxes and things without his name being involved."

"Well, you're the lawyer. I'm sorry about the other. I'll keep looking, but I wouldn't hold out much hope. Another drink?"

"No, I have to get going. I've got a court date tomorrow."

☆   ☆   ☆   ☆   ☆

Over the next few weeks, Egil followed up on the property his client wanted. It was certainly on the market, and when he contacted the real estate agent he seemed more than eager to accept an offer at the price the wolf had mentioned. He had started to draw up the papers for a trust, but the question of ownership still posed a problem. The trust had to have some owner of record. He was reading up on the matter one night when there came a knock at his office door.

"Come in," he said.

The door opened to reveal two men, obviously Native Americans. They both appeared to be in their late forties or early fifties, about six feet and each over two hundred pounds. They were dressed in suits, though they looked more like off the rack at Sears than Saville Row, and wore string ties with silver clips. Neither one looked particularly comfortable in the outfits, as if they were more accustomed to life outdoors than in offices.

"Are you Mr. Njalsson, the lawyer?" the elder of the two asked.

"Yes, that's me. What can I do for you gentlemen?"

"My name is John White Eagle and this is Charlie Loon. We represent the Wolf Lake Band from up north. It's our understanding that you are interested in a certain property in our neck of the woods, and we have a few questions for you, if you don't mind."

"I'll have to hear the questions first. You have to understand that I have to respect the interests of my client."

"But you are interested in buying the old Jensen place? The realtor said as much."

"That much obviously isn't a secret. I have been empowered by my client to purchase the property."

"Could you tell us what your client means to do with it?"

"May I ask why you are so interested? Is there some conflict of title or claim on the property?"

This question seemed to cause a bit of consternation in the two. "Oh, no. It's nothing like that. It's just that, like I said, we represent the Wolf Lake Band. It's not one of your better known tribes. We only have about four hundred members. We've got a little casino. Doesn't make us much money, but it does provide jobs for thirty or forty of our people and a few of the locals. The rest of the tribe mostly survives hunting and fishing like our ancestors. Well, we're just concerned with anything that might interfere with either of those. You can understand that."

By this time White Eagle was sounding downright apologetic. Egil relaxed a little. He was beginning to think that these two, rather than being hired muscle meant to intimidate him, were just two big guys.

"Without revealing too much about my client, I think I can put your minds at rest. My understanding is that my client is only interested in using the property as a kind of retreat where he can spend a few days of each month in seclusion. I am sure he does not want to open a rival casino or do anything else that might be detrimental to the interests of your tribe."

"That does let us breathe easier, Mr. Njalsson. We're a pretty easy going bunch up north, but lately, well there's been some bad stuff going on. Drugs you know, people coming in and growing marijuana or making that meth stuff. They got guns, and not for hunting. Charlie and I, well we're just concerned with keeping everyone safe."

"I can assure you my client is in no way associated with the trade in illegal drugs."

"That's good, then," White Eagle said.

"Is there anything else I can do for you?" Egil asked.

"No. We appreciate your time, Mr. Njalsson," White Eagle replied and started for the door. But before he could reach for the handle, Charlie Loon gave him a nudge.

"Well, there is one more thing. I know you may think this is crazy, but is your client by any chance a wolf?" White Eagle asked this with a sheepish grin and a shrug of his shoulders.

"What exactly do you mean by that?" Egil asked.

"Well, there have been certain rumors. Not everyone believes them, of course, but our people are maybe a little more open to things like that."

"And if my client were a wolf?"

White Eagle looked down at his feet nervously. "Well, if he is, well, then, I would like to say on behalf of the Wolf Lake Band that we are really, really sorry about what happened."

Egil looked at the pair. "I think you gentlemen should take a seat and explain exactly what you are talking about."

"Then your client is a wolf that has been turned into a man?"

"Let's, for the sake of argument you understand, say that that is the case."

"Well, then it's possible, for the sake of argument, that a former member of the Wolf Lake Band may just possible have been responsible. Mind you, this was without the consent and against the desires of the other members of the tribe."

"I find myself very interested in this hypothetical legend. Please go on."

"Well, Charlie here can probably tell it better than I can."

Charlie Loon sat up straight in his chair before he began his tale. "Among the white man there are tales of such a thing as the seventh son of a seventh son. Such a man might have unusual powers. Well, our people also have such a thing. There was a man, a shaman in our tribe. His father had been shaman as had his father and his father before him since long before our people came to these lands from out east. This family of shamans were powerful men, with each shaman passing on his knowledge to his son for generations. You'd call them wizards. These wizards have been part of our tribe, but separate from ordinary men. They pretty much did whatever they wanted, but because they protected the tribe they were tolerated even when they did some bad things.

"Well, the last of these shamans was a man called Harold Bad Moon, and he was the most powerful of all. I won't say he was a bad man, but he would take what he wanted without asking, he drank too much, and he liked to play practical jokes." He said this last as if it was the worst crime ever.

"Well, there was this buck that he had been hunting. He really wanted that buck, but because he drank too much he wasn't having much luck. When he finally caught up with the buck he found this big wolf had got there before him and killed it and was feeding off it. Well Bad Moon, he got mad, and he cursed the wolf. He said that if he wanted a man's deer, then he could be a man. And after that, every full moon the wolf was turned into a man. That same night, though, Harold Bad Moon was crossing the lake in his canoe and it tipped over and he was too drunk to save himself and he drowned."

"Now you have to understand, Mr. Njalsson," White Eagle interrupted. "My people have nothing against wolves and this wolf in particular. They are part of nature, just like the deer and the muskie. And we feel real bad about any inconvenience that may have been caused him. But there is nothing that we can do to change things back. Honest Injun."

"I have to tell you, that the story you've told me pretty much conforms to what my client says. I also want to say that he doesn't appear to bear any ill-will towards your people in general. His main interest is just surviving the periods when he is a man."

"If there is anything we can do, Mr. Njalsson, let us know. We'd be happy to make things right."

"In fact, there is something you can do. I've been working on setting up a trust to maintain the property in question, but there is an issue of who would hold the title. Now if I structured things so that the trust held the property for the Wolf Lake Band, that would solve that problem. I would be named the administrator of the trust to look after my client's interests. I would also structure things so that ownership of the land would revert to the tribe upon the death of my client. Would you find that acceptable?"

Charlie Loon and John White Eagle looked at each other and nodded. "That would be just fine with us, Mr. Njalsson."

"Good. Then I will draw up the papers and consult with my client. I should be able to finalize everything right after the next full moon."

☆   ☆   ☆   ☆   ☆

By the next full moon, Egil had completed the paperwork for the trust and the papers ready for the client to sign. He had them sitting on his desk in front of him when almost as if on cue the were-man knocked on his door.

"Do you have things arranged?" his client asked.

"Yes, all I need is your signature and the funds to pay for the purchase."

The wolf reached inside the light jacket he was wearing and pulling out an envelope handed it to the lawyer.

Egil opened it and examined the contents. It was a certified check for $20,000 drawn on the Justice Department and made out to Egil Njalsson acting for John Q. Wolfe.

"Is it ok?"

"Yes, it seems to be in order. Do you care to tell me how the government came to owe you this much money?"

"It's reward money. I told them about some drug dealers that were using national forest land to grow marijuana and make drugs."

Egil raised his eyebrow. "You don't mess around, do you?"

"They were scaring all the game. Made it hard to hunt. When can I have the cabin?"

"I'll cash this check in the morning. I've already contacted the owner and he's ready to close as soon as the money is available. He seems in a hurry to sell."

"Things have been getting dangerous up there."

"All I need is your signature on these papers. You can write your name, can't you?"

"Yes. And read, too, as I told you earlier. I don't know how. I just can, while I'm a man."

"Good. I've organized things as a trust. Technically, the property will be owned by the Wolf Lake band of Indians.

You will have the use and control of the lands for the next fifty years or until you die. After that, the property reverts to the Wolf Lake Band. Having the title in the name of the Indians simplifies things quite a bit and offers some additional protections that you wouldn't have if you owned it out right. Under the law, the parcel will be considered Indian lands. It also makes it exempt from property taxes. You don't have a problem with that arrangement, do you?"

"As long as I can use the cabin when I need to and nobody bothers me, I'm ok. I don't have a beef with the Wolf Lake people They've never been a problem except that once."

"They're really sorry about that, by the way. Bad Moon, the shaman that cursed you, was acting on his own. They never had much control over his actions."

"About that. You said you were going to talk to someone. See if he could undo the curse so I'd be a wolf all the time."

"Yeah. I asked him about your case. He said there wasn't much he could do without knowing what exact spell was used. And since this Bad Moon is dead, that may not be possible. He's going to do some more research, but he's not holding out much hope. And he'd know if anyone would. He's the best man I know of for traditional forms of magic."

"Well, thanks for trying. Is there anything more for me to do? About the cabin, I mean. Otherwise, I've got to get going. It's a long way back north."

"Are you going to walk all the way back?"

"No. That's a long way. I'll try to hitch a ride."

"Good luck then. I'll leave a copy of the papers at the cabin after the deal is complete"

"Good bye."

☆　☆　☆　☆　☆

It was three in the morning when Egil's phone rang. He picked it up groggily and answered "Who is this?"

The voice on the other end responded in a tired but official sounding manner, "Is this Egil Njalsson the lawyer?" Egil was starting to get real tired of that question.

"Yes it is. Who is this?"

"This is Sheriff Olaf Pederson. Do you know a John Q. Wolfe?"

"Yes, he's a client of mine. What's the matter. Has something happened to him?"

"There's been an incident at a local establishment. Your client was involved. I've got him down at the jail right now."

"Has he been arrested?" Egil said with some alarm.

"No. At least not yet. Maybe not at all. But I'd like to get things sorted out. Is there any way that you could come up here so we could talk in person?"

"I think my calendar is clear this morning," Egil said. Not that he was all that busy. "Just what county are you in?"

The sheriff told him and gave directions. It was about a two hour drive north.

☆   ☆   ☆   ☆   ☆

The Sheriff's department was a door at the back of a courthouse that looked like it had been built as a public works project during the Depression. There were two patrol cars in the parking lot that weren't quite as old, but were a few years shy of being late model. The door opened when Egil tried it. Inside was a large room with a couple of desks, a radio, and the other accessories of a small town police force. A middle-aged man in a uniform was sitting at one of the desks working on a report. He looked up when Egil walked in.

"Mr. Njalsson? Thanks for coming. Would you care for some coffee. It's not good, but it's strong."

"Yes, I'd like that. It's a long drive. How is my client?"

"He's ok. He's taking a nap in one of the cells. He's not under arrest. It's just the only place we had to put him while we waited."

"So what happened?" Egil asked.

"As far as I've been able to piece together, your client, Mr. Wolfe, had been hitching a ride to his place up north and got dropped here in town. He went into a local bar to order something to eat. While he was waiting for his food a couple of local toughs started picking on him about his size. The bartender said he tried to ignore them, but they kept at it. They were pretty drunk. Well, finally one of them went too far, I guess. Your client pushed back and the guy took a swing at him. That's when the fight broke out."

"Is he hurt?" Egil asked. He knew were-wolves were pretty strong and nearly invulnerable while in wolf form, but he didn't have a clue how things worked with a were-man.

"Other than a few cuts, no. I can't say the same for the other two, though. One's got a broken jaw and a dislocated shoulder and a couple of broken ribs, and the other is worse off. Your friend nearly bit his throat out. You wouldn't think he'd have it in him. I mean he can't weigh more than a hundred pounds if that, but he fought like a wild animal."

"It sounds like he was only acting in self-defense, though."

"That's pretty much the way I've got it figured, too. And there were enough witnesses to back him up. The problem is, those two toughs got some friends that aren't too happy. I'm worried about what might happen if I turn your client loose in town here. That's why I was hoping you'd maybe be able to drive him where he's going to avoid any more trouble."

"I might as well. I'm up here anyway, and I do have some business up by Wolf Lake."

"Good. I'm glad that's taken care of. I'll go get your boy for you."

A minute later the sheriff was back with the wolf. His jacket was ripped and there was some blood on his jeans, but he didn't seem the worse for wear.

The sheriff sent them off with a "I wouldn't waste any time getting out of town." Egil got his client into the car and then headed up the highway to Wolf Lake.

It was almost nine by the time they pulled into the little town that hugged the south shore of the lake. There was a tiny diner that served big plates of eggs, bacon, and hashbrowns. While his client was wolfing down his breakfast, Charlie Loon came into the diner for a cup of coffee. If he was surprised to see them he didn't show it. Egil introduced them and they all shook hands around. According to Charlie, the realtor's office was open. While his client was finishing his breakfast, Egil went over to the realtor, closed the deal, and got the keys to the cabin.

He dropped his client off on his way out of town. The cabin wasn't much, mostly a roof and four walls. No electricity, no phone, no driveway out to the road, but then the wolf didn't have a car. He handed him the keys to the cabin and they said their good-byes. Egil didn't expect that he'd ever see the were-man again.

☆　☆　☆　☆　☆

Several months passed, during which Egil's attention was occupied by other matters. The business of the were-man had had receded and been replaced by other cases. He frankly expected that he would never have to deal with it again except for occasional duties related to the trust he had set up.

He was surprised, therefore, when he received a call from Charlie Loon as he worked in his office one afternoon.

"Mr. Njalsson, I thought I'd better tell you that there are some men up here and they're after your client, Mr. Wolfe. They've got guns and I think they mean to kill him."

"Men with guns? Have you told the police?" Egil asked.

"Well, that's just it. There's only the sheriff and a couple of deputies up here. These guys look to be professionals, and if you ask me, not all of them are human."

"Just what do you mean by 'not human'?"

"I'm no shaman, but I picked up a little from my grandfather. I think these guys might be demons."

"Why would demons be after someone who for all intents and purpose is a wolf?"

"It's them drug dealers that he informed on. I think they found out who did it and are out for revenge. There have been rumors going around that the big boss behind the gang is some kind of demon."

"And just what do you expect me to do about it? I'm a lawyer, not a policeman or a demon slayer."

"I don't know. I just thought you should know. Look, we're all scared up here. Bad Moon might have been a drunk and a bully, but he was one heck of a shaman and he always took care of things like this. Now that he went and got himself drowned, we don't have anybody else to turn to. I don't think these guys are going to care one bit if a few Indians get caught in the crossfire. Like I said, I just thought you should know."

"Thanks. And Mr. Loon, if those are demons up there, keep your head down and stay out of their way. You just aren't equipped to fight them."

"Don't I know," the other said before hanging up. Charlie Loon sounded scared, and he had every right to be. The question was, what could Egil do about it. True, he had confronted demons and other denizens of the half world on more than one occasion, but it was not something he relished. Still, he had some obligation to protect his client. What he needed to do was talk to Jack.

Ordinarily, Jack didn't like to talk over the phone. He said that phones were too susceptible to outside influences. Egil suspected that he just wasn't comfortable with modern technology. However, when he found out the cause, he spoke readily enough.

"Do you think it's as bad as he claims?" Jack asked.

"I don't think that Charlie Loon or John White Eagle are the kind of men who scare easily. If they thought they could handle it on their own, they would."

"That's what I was afraid of. It's three days till the full moon. As long as your friend is in wolf form, he's probably safe. Catching a wolf isn't an easy thing, even for a demon. But once he turns into a man, he's going to be in danger. I think we should go up there. How soon can we get there?"

"I was afraid of that. It'll take me a couple of hours to get my gear together. I suspect we should be prepared for a tramp through the woods. Another four or five hours to drive up there. Can you be ready for me to pick you up in two hours?"

"I'll be ready."

☆ ☆ ☆ ☆ ☆

Jack was out on the curb in front of his shop when Egil pulled up. He was dressed in boots, jeans, and a warm jacket like he was ready to go duck hunting. He had his usual bag of goodies where he kept his magical gear. He also had what looked like a gun case. Egil was surprised by that. He had never known his friend to use a fire arm of any sort before. Swords, knives, axes, yes, but not guns.

As Jack got in next to him after stowing his gear in the back seat, Egil noticed that he had made one of his changes in persona. It wasn't anything obvious, but despite the fact that he was still recognizably Jack, he now gave the impression that he was a Native American rather than the Irish gypsy he had been the last few months. The cadence of his speech had changed, too, to reflect the new identity. Egil knew that if he looked, he would find that Jack would be wearing a medicine pouch somewhere on his body. When Jack made one of these transformations he was incredibly thorough about it. He wasn't just wearing a disguise, he had become the new person, in this case, a Native American shaman.

They drove in silence as they headed north. While Jack would talk at length when sitting around his rooms sharing a drink he was never loquacious when on business, but now, as a shaman he seemed even more taciturn than usual. Egil took that as a bad sign. Things were going to get dangerous.

It was nearly midnight when they pulled into the little village of Wolf Lake. It was a clear, crisp night and the full moon was high over head. The only lights on in the village were those of the diner. As Egil wasn't sure he could find his client's cabin in the dark and he wasn't sure what they'd find out in the woods, it seemed a good idea to stop there and see if someone could tell them what was going on.

Fortunately, John White Eagle and Charlie Loon were in the diner talking to a group of men, both white and Native American. One thing they all had in common was the worried looks on their faces. One of the men wore a uniform and a badge and looked even more worried than the others.

John White Eagle looked up to see who the newcomers were. When he saw that it was Egil he came over and greeted them.

"Thanks for coming, Mr. Njalsson. I'm glad you're here. We're worried sick. We heard a bunch of gunfire out in the woods, but to tell the truth, we're all too scared to go out there."

"Any word from my client?" Egil asked. As he wasn't sure how many of the other men in the room were aware of his client's true nature, he thought the neutral reference best.

"Not since these out-of-towners showed up."

"Whose your friend?" Charlie Loon asked, suspiciously. He had joined them by the door. Once they had realized that White Eagle knew them, the rest of the men in the diner had ignored them.

"This is Jack. He's a shaman, a good one. He's here to help."

"I don't recognize the tribe," Charlie said. "You're not from around here, are you?"

"You've heard of the 'Last of the Mohicans?'" Jack responded. "I'm the next to the last, and, no, I'm not from around here."

Something about his manner both assuaged Charlie Loon's suspicions and suggested that he should mind his manners around this new shaman.

"No offense. We're just all on edge."

"None taken," Jack said with a chilling grin.

"I'd like to check up on my client, but I'm not sure I can find his place in the dark. I don't think I should wait until morning," Egil said.

"I can get you out there if you've got a car," White Eagle said. He at least seemed to take heart with the presence of Jack.

"It's right out front."

"Let's go, then. I'll just get my gun." He picked up a shotgun that had been laying on the diner's counter.

They exited the diner. White Eagle got in the front passenger seat while Jack climbed in the rear. Charlie Loon got in on the other side. "I told the others to hang tight till we got back to them."

Once they left the dim light of the village's two street lights the night got incredibly dark. Egil was a city boy, and was used to there always being some light. All he could see was a narrow cone provided by the headlights. The trees on either side of the narrow road seemed to be closing in on them. He was driving at twenty-five and still seemed like he was speeding. At any moment he expected something to pop out of the darkness at them.

At that rate, it took them fifteen minutes to reach the wolf's cabin. Charlie Loon had a big flashlight and led the way on the overgrown path to the cabin.

Egil knocked on the door of the cabin. "Mr. Wolfe? It's Egil Njalsson, your lawyer. Are you in there?"

They could hear a rustling inside the cabin. The door edged open an inch and a luminous eye peered out at them. "Who are the others?"

Egil made quick introductions, "This is Jack, an associate of mine. The other two are John White Eagle and Charlie Loon from the Wolf Lake band. We're here to help."

The manwolf opened the door to let them in. The cabin was dark, but he fumbled with some matches and lit a kerosene lamp. Egil noticed there was a blotch of what looked like blood on the side of his client's shirt.

"Are you ok?"

"I seem to be, now. They shot me. I felt the pain and smelled blood, but when I got back to the cabin it seemed to have healed."

"That's to be expected," Jack said. "When in the were state you possess incredible healing powers, making you practically immortal. However, if the bullet had been silver you would probably be dead now. Of course, once the full moon is over and you revert to your normal form, you will be as vulnerable as any wolf."

"I thought that was just in old movies," Charlie Loon said.

"Much of what is in the movies, the good ones, is true," Jack said. "At least the ones I've been consulted on." They all looked at the shaman in surprise. For all Egil knew, Jack was telling the truth and he had served as a consultant to the movies. Noting about his friend would surprise him at this point.

"That's beside the point, right now," Egil said. "Exactly what happened to you?"

"I was coming back from the lake. I'd been fishing. I heard some noise in the bushes. It sounded like maybe a half dozen men walking slowly and carefully, trying not to make any sound. Next thing I know one of them shouts 'There he is' and there were some shots. That's when they got me. I slinked out of there as best I could in man-shape and headed back here after I had lost them."

"Be glad you were in man-shape," Jack commented. "If you hadn't been, you'd probably be dead now."

"But what happens in a day or two? If what you say is true, once I'm a wolf they can kill me with no problem."

"We'll have to deal with them before that, then," Jack said solemnly.

"Is there anything else you can tell us about these men?" Egil asked.

"Like I said, there were maybe half a dozen of them. I'm not real good with numbers. They all had long guns, and pistols too, I think. And there was something funny about two of them. They didn't smell right."

"What did they smell like?" Jack asked quietly.

"I don't know. Like matches after you light them, I guess."

"Sulfur," Jack said. "You were right when you said they weren't all human. Two of these hunters are demons."

"Demons? How are we supposed to fight demons?" Charlie Loon asked.

"Demons have their weaknesses. They aren't supposed to be in this world. Their proper place is the half world. It takes a lot of energy for them to maintain a presence. It upsets the balance of things. Nature wants to restore the balance. All it needs is a little help which we can give it. That still will leave the four normal men, but I think they won't remain if their backers are forced back into the half world."

"Ok. What do we do to restore the balance?"

"First, we must make some preparations. But we need to act quickly. If it is to be done, it should be done before the moon sets."

"We've got about three hours, then," White Eagle said, but Jack was already removing items from his bag.

He brought out a small drum and beater, a turtle shell rattle, and a long, hatchet shaped pipe which had a raven feather suspended from the bowl. Egil had never seen any of this apparatus before, but then he had rarely seen Jack operate in the persona of a Native American shaman. His own formal training had been mainly in classical European and Norse magics. CalThaum had not been strong on the indigenous aspects of the Art.

"Can either of you drum?" Jack asked Charlie and John.

Charlie replied, "My grandfather taught me some."

Jack handed the drum and beater to him. For some reason he handed the rattle to Egil. From out of his pack, Jack pulled a fur pelt. Egil thought it looked like wolf. He looked at his client. The latter wrinkled his nose and said, "coyote." Jack draped the pelt over his shoulders so that the front paws hung down on his breast. Finally, he took a small pouch of tobacco and filled the bowl of the pipe.

"Are we ready? I need to make the chant to the four winds." Charlie Loon took this as a cue and began a slow beat on the drum. Jack began to chant in a low voice. Carefully, he lit the bowl of the pipe. Then, still chanting, he faced to the north. Egil wasn't sure how he did it, but Jack always seemed to have an unerring sense of direction. For no other reason than it seemed like a good idea, Egil began to shake the rattle in time to the drum.

Jack paused to take a puff on the pipe. He held the smoke a long time and then expelled it in a large cloud to the north. He continued the chant turning counterclockwise to face the west. He repeated the procedure. The tiny room of the cabin seemed to be getting much hazier than the amount of smoke the pipe produced warranted. Egil noticed that John White Eagle was echoing Jack's chant, maintaining the cadence while Jack inhaled the smoke from the pipe. Again the shaman turned, this time to the south. He inhaled, held the smoke for a moment and then blew it out again. His form was starting to become indistinct, as if he was half one thing and half another. Egil wondered if there was something more than tobacco in the pipe.

Finally, Jack turned and faced the east. Once more he took a pull on the pipe, held the smoke, and breathed out. When he had finished, he was no longer Jack. Instead he had taken on the appearance of a creature, half man, half animal, as if he were a coyote standing on two legs.

He handed the pipe and tobacco pouch to John White Eagle. "Do not let it go out until the moon sets." The latter nodded as if he understood the importance.

Jack opened the gun case that he had brought and pulled out a spear. The case was only about three feet long, but the spear was at least six feet long and tipped with a leaf-shaped stone blade. Egil had seen such stone spear points before, in museums where they were labeled Clovis. Not for the first time he wondered just how old his friend actually was.

Taking the spear in his hand, Jack flung the door open and disappeared into the night.

"He's become Coyote," Charlie Loon said, still maintaining the beat on the drum. "My grandfather told me about how some shamans could do that, but I never believed him."

Egil knew enough Native American lore to know that Coyote was a central figure in their mythology. Coyote, the trickster, was a being similar to the Norse Loki, but not inherently evil as Loki was. Whatever his motivation, Coyote was an immensely powerful spirit. Nothing in his training had prepared him for this, for he had a feeling that his friend Jack had not just created an illusion, but that he had, in some way, actually become or invoked the presence of Coyote.

The four of them stood in the smoke filled cabin. Subconsciously, they had each taken up the position of one of the four compass points around the flame of the kerosene lantern. Charlie Loon kept up his drumming, Egil repeated it with the rattle. Periodically, John White Eagle would take a pull of smoke from the pipe and puff it out into the room. The man-wolf stood at his point, eyes wide.

Out in the woods, they could hear that the wind had risen. Occasionally, there would be a shout or a cry from one of the hunters. Except, now they had become the hunted as Coyote led them on his merry chase. Periodically, shots echoed through the forest. The cabin had only one small window, the glass dark from years of dirt, but they could see the gun flashes, first up close, then far away, then nearer again. A shot rang out, then the cry of a man, wounded.

The moon was drawing closer to the horizon. Through the west facing window they could see it just above the tree tops. Still they kept up the beat. There was another shot and a cry, then a third. It now sounded as if only three hunters were active.

Another cry of a wounded man. The moon was now behind the trees, producing a ghostly silhouette. The cries of the hunters were no longer human, but Egil could hear the frustration and anger in those demon voices. They were no match for the power of Coyote.

Finally, the moon had sunk below the horizon. No beam pierced the screen of trees. The forest had gone silent. Not even the normal night sounds could be heard. All animal life had long ago sought shelter from the magical battle that had been going on in those dark woods.

As if by common assent, Charlie Loon stopped his drumming and Egil silenced his rattle. John White Eagle placed the cold pipe on the table next to the lantern. They stood in silence for long minutes, then the door opened.

It was Jack, now just a man with an animal skin draped over his shoulders.

"Egil, me lad," Jack asked in his best Irish brogue. "You wouldn't have any more of that Tullamore dew about you, would you. It's been a long and thirsty night."

Egil pulled a flask out of his jacket pocket and handed it to the wizard.

"Are they gone?" John White Eagle asked.

"The demons are gone. They won't be back, either. The men—well the bodies are out there. One or two might even still be alive. Somehow in the confusion they managed to shoot each other."

"So things are back to normal?" Charlie Loon queried.

"The balance has been restored, if that's what you mean," Jack responded.

"Not quite," the wolf said. "What about me? I still don't want to be a man."

"I haven't forgotten you," Jack said. "I've an idea how the curse might be lifted. But that's a job for another night. Right now I need some breakfast and then a long days sleep."

It was nearly a month later, on the night of the full moon, that Egil and Jack returned to Wolf Lake. During the intervening time, Jack had refused to divulge what he had planned, but on the drive up he given some hints as to what he had in mind.

"It's a question of balance. It came to me while I was running around the woods in the persona of Coyote. Native American beliefs are all about maintaining a balance in nature. When nature is out of balance, bad things happen. That was how I was able to dispel the demons. Their presence in this world destroyed the balance and took an enormous amount of energy. All it took was a little push and that energy drained off and the demons were returned to the half world.

"Now creating a were-creature, of whatever sort, alters the balance of nature. When Bad Moon cursed your client, it created an imbalance. Normally, to undo a curse, you have to know the nature of the curse, or convince the person who authored the curse to undo it. In this case, because of the demise of Bad Moon, neither is possible. He was into some very powerful magics, magics that even I am unfamiliar with."

"So how can we help my client?"

"Well that's where Coyote comes in. This is essentially a problem between the Wolf Lake people and the wolf. Western, or even Eastern methods don't apply. What is needed is to restore the balance between the Wolf Lake Band and the wolf."

"And how do you propose to go about doing that."

"I'm thinking something in terms of a ceremony. A meeting if you will between the members of the Wolf Lake Band and the wolf under a full moon where the band asks for the forgiveness of the wolf and the wolf grants it."

"And you think that will do it?" Egil asked skeptically.

"That's what I'm hoping. And even if it doesn't, I think bringing it out into the open will help to restore the balance so that they all can live in peace."

When they got to Wolf Lake, they drove first to the wolf's cabin to pick him up, and then to the small casino run by the tribe. It took a bit of persuading to get the wolf to accompany them, but when he understood the purpose, he agreed. John White Eagle had arranged, according to Jack's instructions, to gather all four hundred some members of the Wolf Lake Band at the casino.

It was really a very picturesque sight that greeted them at the casino. The casino occupied an old lodge on the lake which had a large lawn big enough to accommodate the gathering. A large fire burned in the center of the lawn, and a few of the older members of the band were off to one side beating on a large drum while some of the younger members dressed in traditional costume danced around the fire. The rest of the band stood around in small groups talking to each other, minding the children or just watching.

They had timed it so that they arrived about ten minutes before midnight, that is midnight by the moon, and not daylight savings time. Jack, Egil, and the wolf approached the fire where John White Eagle and Charlie Loon stood.

"Are you ready?" White Eagle asked.

"Ready as I'll ever be," Jack responded.

"All right then," White Eagle said nervously. "Everybody! Can I get your attention?"

The drummers and dancers stopped and a hush came over the crowd. In the distance frogs could be heard and off across the lake came the cry of a loon.

"You all know that for a while some strange things have been happening around here, ending up with that business last month. Well, we've brought you all together to put an end to it. I don't really understand these things very well, so I've asked Charlie Loon to explain it."

Charlie Loon moved forward a couple of steps. "I don't know that I understand these things any better than John, but here goes. A while back Harold Bad Moon put a curse on a wolf. That was the night he got drunk and drowned himself. Anyway, he cursed this wolf so that every full moon this wolf becomes a man. Now that might not seem so bad, but the wolf doesn't want to be a man. He just wants to be a wolf all the time, which is only natural and right.

"Well, Harold Bad Moon was a member of our band. He was our shaman, and so, even if we didn't ask him to do it, we all, as the Wolf Lake Band, are at fault for this wolf's problems. And this curse had put things out of whack. So to restore the balance we, each and every one of us, has got to ask the wolf's pardon, ask him to forgive us, and maybe if we all do that and he forgives us, the curse will be lifted and the balance restored.

"This fella here," he said indicating the wolf, "is the wolf. Some of you may know him as John Wolfe, but he's really a wolf." This caused a lot of murmuring as not everyone believed the whole story.

"Anyway, this old man here," indicating Jack, "is a powerful shaman. Believe me, I've seen him at work. He says this is the right thing to do, so now is the time for each of us to step up and ask the wolf's forgiveness. Wolf, I'm sorry this happened, it was wrong and I want to make it right."

John White Eagle then spoke up and said, "Wolf, I'm sorry."

There was a moment of silence then an old woman who looked to be about ninety came forward and looked the wolf in the eye and said, "Wolf, I'm sorry."

After that, each member of the band came forward and asked the wolf's forgiveness. When they had all spoken and there were no more coming forward, the wolf stepped out and said, "I know that this wasn't your fault. I don't hold a grudge against the Wolf Lake people. Whether this works or not, I forgive you all."

With that, Jack came up an whispered in the wolf's ear. The wolf began to undress in front of the entire group. Jack looked up at the moon as if to judge the exact moment of midnight. The instant he looked down again the wolf's form began to flow and alter. No longer was he a man, but he had become that which was his nature, a wolf.

The long grey form started to walk towards the forest. The Wolf Lake people parted before him. He walked, not slinked, slowly and confidently. When he reached the edge of the woods he looked back once, and then disappeared into the forest. A little while later there came a long howl from deep in the woods, but it was not a howl of longing, it was a howl of being.

"That's done then, is it?" Charlie Loon asked when the howl had died off.

"I believe so," Jack said. "I think the curse is lifted and the wolf will remain a wolf always."

"Well, after tonight, I don't think any of our people will complain about wolves taking deer or elk. Not around here," John White Eagle said. "On behalf of the Wolf Lake Band I'd like to thank you two for all your help. And if you ever want to come up for a bit of fishing, I know all the best spots."

They shook hands, then Jack said, "I can't keep coming up here every time there's trouble. It's too far. I've know a shaman in the neighborhood. I've talked it over with him and he's agreed to handle all your normal medicine work. Here's his card." He handed a business card to Charlie Loon.

"Come on, Egil, time to get back to civilization." Jack said before heading to the car.

THE POT O' GOLD

THE POT O' GOLD

☆ ☆ ☆ ☆ ☆

It was a gray, late winter afternoon, with icy drops of rain beating against the dingy windows of Egil Njalsson's third story suite in an aging walk-up office building. He was trying to keep his mind on the task at hand, writing a brief describing how a new commercial spell infringed on his client's copyright for an existing spell. It was boring, technically demanding work. It also paid well. Few lawyers had the formal technical training in magic that Egil had acquired with his degree from the California Institute of Thaumaturgy, the legendary west-coast school of metaphysics. His practice these days consisted mostly of writing similar briefs and analyses for other lawyers, who were only too glad to let someone else handle the technical details while they confined themselves to the legal aspects. This was just as well, as the conventional portion of his practice could barely cover the modest rent on his office, let alone provide Egil with a living, and the unconventional part rarely paid at all. Still, even the fact that he was being paid a thousand dollars for a half a day's work was not helping him maintain focus while he detailed the similarity and overlap of two spells whose basic purpose was to ensure the whiteness of ladies unmentionables when used in the approved fashion. It was hardly what he had studied law for.

He was therefore more than a little relieved when he heard a knock on the jamb of the hall door. He had a tendency to leave both the inner and outer doors of his office open while working. It tended to improve the air circulation in the small office at the slight disadvantage of the occasional noise from the cut-rate dentist whose office was on the floor below. And, as he couldn't afford a receptionist, it allowed him to greet the few walk-in clients that came his way.

"Yes? Can I help you?"

"Sure an is this the office of Njalsson the lawyer?" came the reply in a distinct Irish brogue. The fact that the flaking paint on the door proclaimed the same seemed not to be enough.

"It is. Come on in."

Egil waited for the appearance of the prospective client. None appeared. Finally there came the clearing of a throat from somewhere just in front of his desk at a level below the desk top.

The lawyer rose in his chair and looked over the edge of his desk. He blinked his eyes, but that didn't help. If he had been drinking from the bottle of Jameson's that he kept in a file cabinet drawer, it might have explained what he saw. As it was, he felt the urge for a shot.

Standing before his desk was a diminutive man with a ruddy complexion and impossibly red hair poking out from underneath a green derby. He was dressed in what appeared to be a green velvet suit with a wide black belt. A short clay pipe was clenched between his teeth. He was perhaps two feet tall and conformed in every way to the popular conception of a Leprechaun. Somehow, Egil felt that he was not, in fact, a midget.

"How can I help you, Mr. —?" Egil asked.

"Seamus O'Shaunesy. First, you could offer me a seat so that we can look each other in the eye without the craning of our necks. Second, are you Njalsson?"

"Please have a seat, Mr. O'Shaunesy," Egil said motioning to his one chair reserved for visitors. The client clambered up into the chair, but it provided little improvement. The addition of a two volume dictionary and Blackstone's Commentaries remedied the situation.

Once they were both seated again, Egil answered "I'm Njalsson."

"The attorney-at-law who does magic?"

"If by that you mean the lawyer who is a certified and licensed wizard, then yes, I am that Njalsson."

"The word going around is that you know what you're about when it comes to such matters and that you are not afraid of taking a client that isn't, shall we say, strictly human."

"I try to keep an open mind in such matters," Egil agreed. "My main concern is with the justice of the case."

"Put in a very lawyerly way, Mr. Njalsson. That's good enough fer me. It just so happens that I have a wee bit of a legal problem which I could use your help with."

"Well it's loik this," O'Shaunesy said. As he relaxed his brogue seemed to deepen. "I am by way of being the proprietor of a first class saloon named fittingly enough 'The Pot O' Gold'. A foin little establishment. None of that jukebox music or televisor screens blarin' sporting events. Jest good dark beer and whiskey that's not watered. I inherited the place from me da, Shaun O'Shaunesy, and we've been servicing the working man's thirst for over eighty years."

"It sounds like a very reputable establishment, Mr. O'Shaunesy. Just what is the problem?"

"It's the wee matter of the license. Now the place has been licensed since the end of prohibition, it was a speakeasy before that, and we never had no problem with the license, but when I went to renoo it this year, the application was denied. Well, even a Leprechaun can't run a saloon without a license these days."

"Did they give grounds for denial?"

"That, sir, they did not. They gave me some double talk about it being in abeyance and that there was a motion of condemnation under eminent domain against the property. Well that was the first I'd heard of that."

"That usually means that the city is taking the property for development purposes. But they would have to offer you fair compensation. Have you received any such offers."

"Well there was some fool come around trying to buy the place and get me to sign some papers. I told O'Toole to toss him out on his ear."

"O'Toole?" Egil enquired.

"That's me bouncer. He's six foot six and weighs eighteen stone. Not much trouble with O'Toole around."

"I see. Go on."

"Well the next thing I know I've got this summons and the city is threatening to close me down by Friday. And that's with St. Patrick's day less than three weeks away. That's me biggest night of business," O'Shaunesy exclaimed.

"I'd like to see the summons if you have it with you?"

"I've got it roight here," O'Shaunesy said, reaching into his inside jacket pocket. He produced a couple of folded papers and handed them to the lawyer.

Egil looked them over. It was about what he expected.

"The summons is on a charge of assault against a public official. It seems the fool that you tossed out was from the city attorney's office and that he was trying to negotiate a settlement as part of the condemnation proceedings. The other is a notice of a hearing to revoke your license on the grounds that you are running a disorderly house."

"It's nothin' of the sort. We didn't even allow women in the place until they made us."

"I think they are referring to the tossing of the attorney and not to prostitution," Egil corrected.

"That's different. I was insulted there for a minute. Well, can you fix it? And how much will it cost?"

"I'll be honest with you, Mr. O'Shaunesy. These are rather serious charges. Unless I can prove that the city wasn't following proper procedures there may not be much that can be done."

"But you're a wizard, man. Can ye not put a wee hex on 'em to make 'em forget the whole business?"

"I'm afraid that wouldn't be ethical," Egil answered. "Also, I doubt it would be effective. I think a much better approach would be to find out who's behind this condemnation and see if the city has crossed all their *t*'s and dotted their *i*'s."

"Ye do, do ye?"

"Yes, I do," Egil said. "That's my professional opinion. I have dealt with a similar case and I did have some success."

"Was the client a Leprechaun?"

"No, in fact he was a vampire."

O'Shaunesy shuddered. "Did you win his case?"

"Yes. Unfortunately, my client expired shortly thereafter. But that had nothing to do with the legal aspects of the case."

"That's reassuring," O'Shaunesy said with a sigh. "Well, will you take the case, Mr. Njalsson?"

"I'll tell you what, Mr. O'Shaunesy. I'll look into a few things and see if there is anything I can do. If not, I won't charge you. If I find I can help you, we can talk about the arrangements then."

"Fair enough."

"Where can I reach you?"

"Ye can always find me at the Pot O' Gold. I live in the flat above when the saloon's not open."

"Good. I'll let you know one way or the other in a day or two."

"Thank you, Mr. Njalsson. You're a real gentleman."

With that, O'Shaunesy clambered off Blackstone and the chair, tipped his hat and strode out of the office.

☆   ☆   ☆   ☆   ☆

It was after seven by the time Egil had finished the brief, in part because his mind kept being pulled away by the problems posed by the leprechaun, which if nothing else were more interesting than those raised by laundry spells. He felt the need to talk, and so, after stopping for a six pack of Guinness at the corner liquor store, he headed to the one person who was sure to have some knowledge about the subject.

Jack Smith, a.k.a. Jakob Schmitz, or whatever name he was going by these days maintained a small second hand shop on the poor side of town. The stock of the shop never seemed to turn over and Egil knew it mainly served as a cover for a small time sideline in fortune telling and love potions. Egil had defended Jack in a case of practicing magic without a license a few years earlier. He'd lost the case but made a friend. He had also discovered that while the old man might lack credentials he probably knew more of the Art then the entire faculty at Call Thaum.

Where or when Jack had acquired this knowledge had never been made clear. Not that Jack kept his past a secret, but the stories he told seemed so wild and improbable that they were hard to believe. He had claimed by turns to have studied at the Sorbonne in Egypt; Tibet, amongst native

American shamans and with the gypsies of Transylvania. Some of the stories could only be true if they had occurred in the last century or even earlier. On the other hand, the old man did seem to have a working knowledge of the magical lore of all of those cultures and dozens more besides.

The sign in the shop window said "closed" when Egil arrived, but he rang the bell anyway. Jack lived in a small apartment above the shop and had a sort of consultation room behind it. After a minute or so a small bearded face peered out from behind the glass in the door. He unlocked the latch, made a small hand flourish to undo the protection spell and opened the door.

"So what brings my favorite lawyer calling at this hour?" Jack asked.

"I felt the need for some company and conversation."

"It's better for you than television. Come in. I see you've brought refreshments," Jack said motioning towards the brown paper bag in Egil's hand.

"Guinness," Egil explained.

Jack raised his eyebrow.

"It seemed appropriate," Egil shrugged.

"You'd know best. Have a seat in the parlor. I'll get some glasses."

The consulting room was familiar to Egil. There was a small table in the center covered with a green baize table cloth. On the table, under a covering of black velvet, was, he knew, a crystal ball. Two walls of the room were occupied by massive bookshelves reaching to the ceiling. They contained not only every contemporary text on magic in a half dozen languages but works on physics, mathematics, chemistry and astronomy. There were also hundreds of older books in Latin, Greek, Hebrew, and other languages, grimoires, spellbooks, and other magical texts some of which were not even supposed to exist. How or when Jack had come by them was a mystery. A third wall of the room was covered in photos ranging from modern snapshots to ancient tintypes. They showed scenes from all over the world, Europe, Tibet, the Great Plains in the nineteenth century. Curiously, in each and every one of them, there was a figure that could, with a little imagination be Jack. The fact that the figure was variously a Lakota shaman, Tibetan monk, Irish gypsy or whatever just deepened the mystery.

Egil didn't have time to ponder the question as Jack returned with a brace of pint glasses which he ceremoniously filled from the beer Egil had brought. The foamy white head wasn't as good as one could get from a keg, but it was not bad.

"So what is it you want to talk about?" Jack asked once he had settled himself in a chair.

"Leprechauns."

"That explains the Guinness. Or perhaps it's the other way around. Why the sudden interest in the subject? Norse trolls and dwarves always seemed more in your line." Egil was proud of his Norse heritage and never made a secret of it. He even tended to favor it in his magic.

"I may have a new client. He owns a saloon called 'The Pot O' Gold.' If he's not a leprechaun he certainly looks the part."

"The Pot O' Gold?" Jack exclaimed. "They make a great corn beef sandwich. And yes I know corned beef isn't really Irish, but it's still a good sandwich. What has O'Shaunesy been up to?"

Egil explained the situation.

"That's too bad. It's a great saloon. What do you want to know?"

"Well, I guess first of all, is O'Shaunesy really a leprechaun?"

"He says he is," Jack affirmed. "I have no reason to doubt him. You don't have any prejudice against the wee people, do you lad?"

"No. It's just that I've never had any contact with leprechauns before. It's a little out of my line. That's why I wanted to know what you could tell me. I want to know what I'm getting myself into."

"Well, you know that the British Isles and Ireland in particular are one of those places where the boundaries between this world and the half-world are a bit soft. It's been that way at least since they put up Stonehenge and New Grange." Jack said that as if he'd been there when they applied for the building permit.

"Anyway, there has always been a bit of crossover between the two worlds, pixies, fairies, banshees, tinkers, gypsies and such. And of course, leprechauns. There just seems to be something about the Celtic soul that is more receptive to such creatures than other peoples. And where the Irish go, so the wee people follow. There's more of them about than you'd believe. They just have a knack for going unnoticed when they want to."

"Running a saloon wouldn't seem to be maintaining a low profile," Egil commented.

"Ah, but who's going to believe a drunk?"

"Point taken," Egil said as he sipped his stout.

"Now other than an ability to be elusive, leprechauns aren't really particularly magical. Back in the old country, they mostly got by on handouts, shoe-making and pot mending and the like. You have to remember that Ireland was a poor country. The Famine hit the wee folk as hard as it did the rest of the population, which is why so many emigrated with the rest of the Irish."

"The New World now, well, that presented a whole new set of possibilities. There were fortunes to be made, work to be found. You think all those Pony Express riders were young boys?"

"Leprechauns?"

"Them or fairies. Pixies were just a little too small to pull it off. Anyway, some made it big, some went broke, and some just hung around. Now the way I heard it, Shaun O'Shaunesy made his fortune during prohibition. He took his ability at being elusive to good use running whiskey down from Canada. He used the proceeds to set himself up with a saloon. Finally, his longing for the old sod got the better of him and he returned to Ireland leaving the Pot O' Gold to his son Shamus."

"Okay," Egil said. "What about this pot of gold business?"

"That's mostly just old wives tales. Like I said, a lot of the leprechauns picked up a little cash mending shoes and pots and things. Well, Ireland was a poor country, and anyone with three shillings to his name was a rich man. There were always those who were willing to risk the wrath of the wee folk by depriving them of their hard earned money. Of course, leprechauns being what they are, few ever succeeded. The Irish being who they are, the stories got multiplied in the telling and every leprechaun came, in the public imagination, to possess a vast fortune in gold which was buried in a pot somewhere."

"It's not true then?"

"Oh, I won't say it was never true, but most of the gold buried in Ireland was left there by your ancestors, the Vikings, and not by leprechauns."

"So from what you're saying, there probably isn't a magical aspect to this case except for the fact of O'Shaunesy being a leprechaun."

"I've never known him to use magic in his saloon. I know that," Jack said. "Speaking of which, is there another Guinness in that bag of yours?"

Egil handed a can to the old wizard and opened one for himself.

"So all I really need to worry about are the normal legal aspects of the case."

"I didn't say that," Jack corrected. "What I did say is that O'Shaunesy doesn't use magic. What the people interested in his property might do is still an open question. You've seen enough dubious activity by unscrupulous developers in this town to know that there are some that won't hesitate to use whatever means they have at their disposal to carry out their schemes. That could be magic, vampires, demons or whatever."

"That's reassuring," Egil said.

"That's life in our fair city."

They spent the rest of the six pack discussing various aspects of Irish magical lore, none of which seemed applicable to the matter at hand. It was still early, just after ten, when Egil left. He realized he hadn't eaten yet, so he headed to a diner near his office that he frequented.

The diner was close to the main police station and many of the regulars were officers going on or coming off a shift. He arrived at the diner just after the transition from the evening to the graveyard shift, so he wasn't surprised when he saw his friend Joe O'Neil at the counter, a hamburger and cup of coffee sitting in front of him.

"Hi, Joe. Anything new?" he said as he grabbed the stool next to the patrolman.

"Same old, same old; drunks, family spats, and juvenile delinquents. What's my favorite shyster up to these days?"

"I'm defending a leprechaun. Owns a bar called the 'Pot O' Gold'. Know it?"

"Are wild bears Catholic? The 'Pot O' Gold' is a fine saloon. I hope O'Shaunesy hasn't gotten himself in too much trouble."

"Has everyone been to this place except me?" Egil asked with exasperation.

"It would seem that way, councilor. A lot of us boys in blue go there when we want to let off steam. Many's a bachelor party and wake been held there."

"Maybe not for much longer," Egil commented.

"Say it ain't so," he responded.

"The city wants to shut it down. Word is some developer wants to build on the block. There's a condemnation motion in progress and their trying to take away the license to serve because O'Shaunesy popped someone from the city's attorney's office when he tried to negotiate a settlement."

"That would be a real shame. The 'Pot O' Gold' is a real old fashioned saloon. Sawdust and peanut shells on the floor, no juke box, no televisors. O'Shaunesy treats all his customers the same way, badly, but the beer is good and the prices are fair. Can't ask for more than that these days."

"Don't expect you can. Sounds like I should get over there while I can."

"I'd do that. They make a great corned beef sandwich. And yes I know it ain't Irish."

"Maybe I'll head over there right now," Egil said.

"Sounds like a plan. I'd join you but the wife is expecting me," O'Neil remarked. "Seriously. Anything that you can do to keep the place open would be appreciated by us flatfoots."

"I'll keep that in mind," Egil said as he got up to leave.

☆   ☆   ☆   ☆   ☆

The Pot O' Gold wasn't that far from the diner—less than a dozen blocks. It didn't look like much of a place from the outside. There was a sign with the name across the front above the door and a couple of beer signs and a neon shamrock in the front windows. Inside, it was different—a long deep room stretching back into the gloom. A mahogany bar ran along one side of the room while a number of booths were arranged on the other. Towards the back a dart board hung dangerously near the door to the men's restroom.

One curious feature was a narrow walkway that ran behind the length of the bar at just the right height for O'Shaunesy to interact with his customers on a face-to-face basis. The effect was much like a castle's fortification with the leprechaun shielded by the crenellations formed by tap handles, racks of peanuts, and jars of pickled eggs. Nothing in the bar looked as if it was younger than fifty years including the eggs.

The crowd seemed light to Egil—mostly men standing at the bar looking as if they were there because they had nowhere else to go.

O'Shaunesy saw him, waved and cried out, "I'd like to talk, councilor, but I've a bit of a crisis at the moment."

"Oh?" Egil asked curiously.

"Yeah. Somethin's happened to the beer. The temperature is all wrong. The porter is coming out with icebergs and the lager tastes like warm dishwater."

"That sounds bad. Maybe I can help."

"Thanks councilor, but it doesn't strike me as a legal matter," the Leprechaun responded.

"Is it only the kegs?"

"Yeah," the Leprechaun answered suspiciously. "The bottles and cans are fine, but my margins are half what they are for taps. I'll go broke before they close me down at this rate."

"Your kegs have the standard temperature control spell on them, I assume?"

"Of course. You know about that kind of thing?"

"It's one of the first things they teach in industrial magic class."

The spell to maintain the temperature of beer kegs from the brewery to the bar had been one of the first spells to be commercially successful. It dated to the middle of the nineteenth century. Legend had it that it had been developed by Helmholz himself when he couldn't get his favorite beer in the summer due to the German Beer Purity laws. With it a brewer could insure that a keg was maintained at a temperature appropriate to the style of beer from the time it was released until it was consumed. Bar owners loved it because it saved them the expense of having to have extra refrigerated space for kegs and that they could serve dark beers such as stouts at one temperature and light lagers at another. Unfortunately, no one had yet come up with a cost effective spell for smaller containers such as bottles and cans.

"Well if you can help, you can have free beer for life. And those that know me know I don't make such promises lightly."

"Where are your kegs?"

"This way. The door to the cellar is at the back end of the bar." The leprechaun led the way nimbly dodging glassware and bottles on the walkway. At the end there was a hole in the floor with a leprechaun sized ladder. A narrow stairway was next to it for those of a more normal size.

The cellar was about what one might expect in a hundred year old building, dark, and damp, though surprisingly clean. Kegs were arranged in orderly rows with the plumbing necessary to tap them arranged conveniently overhead. Each tapped keg had a replacement already in place for when it was empty.

As Egil examined the kegs he noted the seal and stamp of the spell provider on each along with the guaranteed temperature. Sure enough, as he felt the tap line on a keg of Guinness he could tell that the contents were ice cold rather than the fifty five degrees the spell promised.

He didn't normally carry his bag of magic apparatus with him, but he always made sure to have a few supplies stored in his jacket pockets. He drew a glass rod from one of them and gave it a quick wave. Instantly, it burst into a bright, white glow which he used to exam the surface of the keg. It didn't take him long to find what he was looking for. Satisfied, he checked another keg to confirm his suspicions.

O'Shaunesy stood by expectantly. "Did ya find somethin', councilor?"

"See this?" Egil asked.

"Looks like some chalk marks to me."

"It's a spell. Written in Ogham. It's an old Celtic form of writing which uses a vertical or horizontal line with various numbers of intersecting lines to represent the various letters of the alphabet."

"Irish, you say?"

"Yes. The spell disrupts the temperature reference of the breweries spell. That's why the beer comes out at the wrong temperature."

"Who would do such a thing? And good beer too."

"It's hard to say. The spell itself isn't complex, but it's been written in an unusual language—Old Elfish."

"Those pointy eared varmints," O'Shaunesy cursed, ignoring the sharp angles at the top of his own ears.

"Just because it's in Elfish doesn't mean it was done by an Elf. I can read it for instance."

"Well, we can fix it, though, can't we—if we just wipe out the marks?" He reached out to wipe the nearest keg, but Egil intercepted him.

"It's not quite that simple. The marks are endowed with a certain amount of power. Attempting to erase them might have unintended consequences."

"Such as?"

"The kegs might explode."

"Oh," the leprechaun said, looking crestfallen. "Well what can we do?"

"Let me think a minute," Egil said.

After a bit he asked, "Is there any chalk down here?"

"Over there," the leprechaun said pointing at a chalk board on which the various kinds of beer kegs were tallied.

Egil retrieved the piece of chalk that was used for the tallying and made a sample mark on one of the kegs.

"As I suspected, they used chalk that they found here. They probably didn't want to be traced by it."

"You mean they moidered me own beer with me own chalk?"

"I'm afraid so. But that's actually good for us. Now let's see. Yes, that should do it." He began making marks on the keg of Guinness, adding a line here and there to the existing letters and putting some additional characters at the beginning and end of the spell.

"I've changed the spell so that it says something completely different. It now says, well, never mind. It's better that you don't know. In any case, the beer should now be at the right temperature."

"You're sure?"

"Try it," Egil answered.

"Liam," O'Shaunesy bellowed up through the stairwell, "Pull a point of Guinness from tap number one. Tell me how it tastes."

They waited a few minutes while the pint was pulled. A large ruddy face appeared in the stairwell holding the glass of dark liquid. "It's foin, Boss. Jus' the right temp." As if to prove his point he took a long swig of the stout. The thick foam was evident on his smiling face.

"Back to work, with ye' then," O'Shaunesy yelled. "Can you fix the others?"

"No problem," Egil replied. "It should only take me a few minutes. It looks as if they only marked the kegs that were tapped and the ones that were queued up to replace them. The others look like they are ok."

"Thank the saints for small favors. I might never have known. Well I'll leave you to it then, councilor. And I'll have a bit of refreshment waiting for you when you're done."

It was more like fifteen minutes before Egil had redone all of the spells. When he emerged from the cellar there was a pint of stout and a corned beef sandwich waiting for him, O'Shaunesy beaming behind the bar. Oddly the sandwich was made with Jewish rye. It didn't matter, it was, as advertised, quite good.

The next time he saw Jack he related the details of the incident with the beer. The wizard seem surprised and a little bit troubled.

"It's pretty unusual for Elfish to be used in magical spells, especially written in Ogham characters. That's old country lore, not the sort of thing they teach wizards these days. In fact, I'm a little surprised that you could read it well enough to counter the spell."

"I always did have an interest in obscure languages and scripts. I had a professor at Cal Thaum that was a real nut on the subject. He taught a great intro course on the subject. It was kind of the rage when I was in college. Of course, it wasn't part of the regular curriculum."

"So you learned something in that fancy school after all. Still, the use of Elfish would seem to hint at some sort of halfling connection."

"I've never run into an elf before. Do you think one could be behind O'Shaunesy's troubles?"

"By custom and treaty they keep to the half world. The elves are a strange race, but honorable. They tend to keep their word. They also rarely show any interest in human matters. They feel it's beneath them. Still, elves and leprechauns have never gotten on well together. That's part of the reason you see so many of the latter on this side."

"I have to admit," Egil said, "that I'm not as familiar with this particular area of the Lore as I might be. It doesn't come up much."

"That's something we should remedy, lad. I think I've got a book somewhere that might just be up your alley. It might be of use in your current predicament, as well."

Jack began to search through the contents of his bookshelves. While there was a rough sort of order to the collection, there were so many odd volumes that things tended to get tucked where they fit best by size rather than subject. Finally he came up with a small volume. Blowing the dust off it he handed it to Egil.

"Of course, it's a translation, but it is fairly accurate," the elder wizard said.

Egil opened it up to the title page, noted that it was in Latin and had been printed in 1835 in Dublin. The title was

The Laws and Customs of Faerie, with Commentary, Translated by Fra. Jack O'Higgins.

"I know, it's before the modern era, when magic was still the Art and not yet a Science, but it's sound, nevertheless—at least when it comes to dealings with Elves."

"Well if elves are involved, this looks like it might be useful. May I take it with me?"

"I wouldn't have handed to you otherwise, Egil. Just take care of it. I'm not sure if I could find another copy. I've had this one quite awhile."

Egil didn't doubt that. Half of Jack's collection seemed to date from previous centuries. He thumbed through the volume when he got back to his apartment. To his astonishment, it was after three before he could put it down.

☆　　☆　　☆　　☆　　☆

He was working in his office a few days later when he got a call from Joe O'Neil.

"Hi, Joe. What's up?"

"I was wondering if you could meet me after my shift tonight. There's someone that wants to talk to you. It has to do with the Pot O' Gold."

"I can make it. At the diner around the usual time all right?"

"That would be splendid, councilor. I'll see you then," O'Neil said as he hung up.

The call puzzled Egil. Joe rarely called him out of the blue. Also, it seemed to the lawyer that the policeman had been sounding particularly Irish over the phone.

☆　　☆　　☆　　☆　　☆

When he got to the diner he found Joe had claimed one of the booths. There was a man sitting across the table from him. Egil thought he recognized him as a detective on the force.

"I'm not interrupting anything, am I?" Egil asked as he approached the booth.

"Not at all, at all. The fact is we've been waiting for you. This is Liam Collins. He's a detective on the fraud squad."

Egil didn't need to hear the name to know that the detective was another Irishman. He was a lean figure with fair skin and dark red hair and features that just screamed of the old sod.

"I understand that you've been hired by O'Shaunesy," the detective said after Egil had slid into the booth next to O'Neil.

"He's retained me to deal with some legal problems," Egil said cautiously.

"You have to understand, councilor, that there are a lot of people in the department that are rather fond of the Pot O' Gold. Especially those of us that are of Irish descent."

"So I've gathered from Joe."

"Well, we'd take it hard if the place was to close," Collins said.

"I'm sure that my client appreciates your support."

"Well, it just so happens that I might have some information that could prove useful to you."

"And what might the nature of this information be?"

"You see, it's like this. I'm on the fraud squad. Well a lot of investigations of commercial matters come under that heading. I've been investigating one Charles "the Rat" Feeney. He claims that he's a real estate developer, but we got suspicions that he might be involved in some other things. Things like laundering money."

Egil wasn't really surprised. He'd come up against plenty of developers who were willing to work outside the law before, and as many corrupt officials in the city government who were only too willing to help them.

"I've been on a detail that's been conducting surveillance of Feeny. I've noticed some interesting things. I wasn't sure what it meant until I heard about the incident with the beer."

"Oh?" Egil queried.

"I've got some photos here you might be interested in seeing." Collins reached down on the bench next to him and brought up a folder marked "Police Department, Confidential."

"Here's a picture of Feeney."

Egil could see that he hadn't gotten his nickname just because of his personality. He had a short squinty face with a narrow pointy nose that gave the impression of a rodent in his ancestry. In the picture Feeney was looking around him suspiciously as he was in the act of flicking a cigarette butt on the sidewalk.

"OK. It's these next photos that are the interesting part," Collins said as he spread two 8x10's on the table. "These two have been seen in association with Feeney that last couple of months. We suspect that they've been doing some of his dirty work."

Egil took a good long look at the two photos. Both of the men shared common characteristics. They were tall—over six feet—but thin of build, almost too thin. They both had shoulder length hair that was almost white. The photos were in black and white but despite the light hair, they appeared to have swarthy complexions. One of them was holding a cigarette in fingers that were extremely long and thin. But the most telling feature of all was that both men had ears that came to distinct points. Unless he was mistaken, they were definitely elves.

"These two appeared seemingly out of nowhere about three months ago. Before that, nothing. No record here or anywhere else as far as we've been able to uncover. It's like they just popped out of thin air."

"Or out of the half world," Egil commented.

"That was my thought, exactly," Collins said. "I think these guys are elves."

"Swart elves, to be precise," Egil clarified. "You can tell by the complexion. They're a sort of lower order than the high elves. They've got a nasty reputation for treachery even on the other side."

"They're getting a reputation around town, too. Extortion, intimidation. They seemed to have hooked up with Feeney and have been trying to persuade people on the same block as the Pot O' Gold to sell out cheap. Problem is, we haven't been able to catch them at it."

"Not surprising. Elves are known for their ability for stealth."

"Invisibility?" Collins asked.

"No, they just can make themselves very hard to notice. That's probably how they got into the cellar at the Pot O' Gold to sabotage the beer."

"Yeah. I thought it was something like that. A guy that ran a grocery down the block had all his dairy product go rancid on him. That was after he refused to sell. He changed his mind after that. There wasn't anything we could do. No proof."

"I appreciate the information, Liam, but what do you expect me to do with it?" Egil asked.

"I don't know. Maybe nothing. But I thought you should know. We figure that if these two were out of the picture, Feeney might not have a strong hand to play."

"What else can you tell me about these two?"

"Not much. Here's the file we got on them. It's pretty skimpy." He passed a couple of sheets from the folder over so Egil could look them over.

Collins had been charitable when he had called them skimpy. There was an address of an apartment where they evidently were living. There were the names that they were using, obviously false as they were "Smith" and "Jones." There were also a couple of aliases. It was the last of these that caught Egil's attention. They didn't fit with the others. They weren't typical American names. In fact they sounded distinctly Elvish.

"Are you certain about these?" Egil said pointing at the names.

"We think so. We caught them in a private conversation with a long distance bug." He was describing a spell that allowed a conversation to be heard at a distance, a typical police surveillance tool. "I'm not sure of the spelling, but we got them on tape. Why? Is it important?"

"It might be. It just might be. If you could get me a copy of that recording, it would be useful."

"It's against department policy," Collins said. "But then, showing these photos to you is against policy, too. I'll see what I can do."

"Whatever you can do."

"So do you see an angle that we can get to this Smith and Jones?" Collins asked.

"Maybe. I've got to look up a point of law or two first, though."

"See. What did I tell you, Liam. The councilor here is just the guy that can get things done when it comes to the magical."

"Well, it would sure be a shame if O'Shaunesy lost the saloon. If there's anything I can do, let Joe know. He can get in touch with me." Collins gathered up the photos and papers and stuffed them back in the folder. He shook Egil's hand and then left.

"So, councilor. It looks to me that you've got an idea hatching in the back of your head."

"Maybe, Joe. Just maybe."

☆   ☆   ☆   ☆   ☆

The next few days found Egil very busy. First he had to deal with his client's immediate legal problems. Fortunately, his conversation with Collins had given him a handle on the charge of assaulting the man from the city attorney's office. Several businessmen on the same block as the Pot O' Gold had filed reports with the police alleging extortion attempts on the part of Smith and Jones. He was able to argue that his client had mistaken the city man for an extortionist and had acted accordingly. Surprisingly, the D. A. was sympathetic and the charge was dropped. That still left the issues of the liquor license and condemnation proceedings, but hopefully those would clear up if Feeney and his elves where taken care of.

Most of his time, however, was spent in reading and digesting the book that Jack had lent him. Understanding an unfamiliar legal system is never easy, as in the law so much depends on precedent and case law. When the legal system originates from the half world the task is doubly difficult. The fact that he was studying a translation of the original written in a rather elaborate nineteenth century Latin didn't help matters, Still, after several days of study, Egil thought that he had discovered a strategy that would remove the two elves from the scene, and with them, any magical support that Feeney enjoyed.

It was time to run his idea past Jack, and as he felt the occasion called for something more cerebral than beer or ale, he armed himself with a quart of the best Irish whisky he could find. Jack ushered him into his back room and produced a pair of appropriate glasses.

"So what is it you have in mind, lad?" Jack said as he pulled the seal from the bottle and poured three fingers of the amber liquid in each glass.

"As I see it, these two elves are the key to the problem. Without them, Charles Feeney is just a two bit hustler. The question is, how do we get rid of them. I don't relish the idea of going up against them in a magical duel."

"That's wise of you, for sure. Two elves, even of the lower orders, are forces to be reckoned with," Jack concurred.

"But even elves, particularly in this world are subject to the Law," Egil countered, his voice emphasizing the capital on the last word.

"And which law would that be? Clearly these two wouldn't be subject to human law."

"No, they wouldn't. But there is a law that would bind them, and that is a treaty signed by the King of Fairie, Oberon himself."

"I begin to see your point. Is there such a treaty?"

"There is signed between Oberon and Brian Boru himself back in—well, whenever it was that it was signed. Oberon and Brian, acting as the King of Faerie and the High King of Tara respectively, signed a treaty known as the 'Grand Compact' restricting incursions on the part of the elves into the mundane world. In the compact, Oberon promises to punish any elf that violates the boundary or causes 'various mischiefs in any human countrie.'"

"And you think that Oberon would still honor this compact? It's been a long time since the days of Brian Boru."

"The way I see it," Egil explained, "these two swart elves are probably renegades from Fairie already. I suspect that Oberon or his agents would only be too glad to get their hands on them."

"All well and good, lad. But how are you planning on delivering these two to Fairie?"

"I've a plan to take them by ambush. I've got a good half dozen or more of the city's finest that have agreed to aid me. With them and the force of cold forged iron I think that I can neutralize the elves magic powers long enough to open a portal into the half world and send them through."

"And what's to keep them from just returning when the conditions are right?"

"That's the weak spot in the plan. If only there was a way to get a message through to the Court of Oberon to have an agent waiting on the other side of the portal."

"I might be able to arrange that," Jack said. "But Oberon has a reputation for being touchy about his prerogatives. Any such message would have to be couched in the proper format."

"I've thought about that. I've got a rough draft here with me. If you could look it over an tell me what you think?"

Egil pulled out a paper from his inside coat pocket and handed it to the elder wizard.

After several minutes studying the document he nodded and said, "You can tell you're a lawyer, lad. I couldn't have done better, meself. The phrasing is just such as to flatter Oberon into agreement. Are you sure you've got the true names of your 'Smith' and 'Jones' down right? You're whole scheme may depend on that."

"I have a recording of them pronouncing the names in their own voices. I have it here."

Egil produced a portable recording sphere and played back the conversation Collins had given him.

"You and your friends have done good work," Jack said with a nod. "When do you plan to spring your trap?"

"In two days under the next full moon. The barriers to the half world will be at their weakest then."

"And how will you lure these two? They are sure to be on their guard."

"I've arranged a meeting between O'Shaunesy and Feeney, ostensibly to discuss terms for selling the Pot O' Gold. I figure that Feeney won't show up without the two elves for protection."

"It's a bold plan, lad, but I think it could work. Would you mind a little extra help from an old man?"

"I was counting on it, Jack," Egil said.

"Then let's drink to our success," Jack said as he refilled their glasses.

"Slange."

☆   ☆   ☆   ☆   ☆

They had agreed to meet at the Pot O' Gold at eleven before proceeding to the meeting place. Joe O'Neil was there with Liam Collins. Accompanying them were eight of the biggest, beefiest cops Egil had ever seen.

"Sons of Ireland, every one of them," O'Neil said. "Except for Kowalski, there at the end. He just likes good beer."

"Do you all know what is involved?" Egil asked. "You'll be going up against two renegade elves. They are bound to be armed and dangerous."

"I've explained it all to them, councilor," O'Neil said. "They're all ready to put it on the line for the Pot O' Gold."

"I'm ready, too," came a voice from behind the bar. O'Shaunesy was standing up on the bar brandishing a lethal looking knobkerrie walking stick. "I'll show those pointy-eared rascals. Think they can take me Pot O' Gold, do they?"

"Ok," Egil said. Here's the plan."

☆   ☆   ☆   ☆   ☆

The chosen meeting place was a vacant lot not far from the Pot O' Gold. The fact that Feeney saw nothing unusual about meeting at midnight in such a place was almost a proof that he was not playing on the up and up. Only a criminal would feel comfortable in such a forbidding location.

Egil and his group arrived early so that he could position the policemen. They needed to be out of sight, but close enough that they could come in at the proper moment. It had been agreed with Feeney that only two people would accompany each principal. In the case of O'Shaunesy, Egil and Jack were to be with him. Egil was fairly certain that the two elves, Smith and Jones, would be backing up Feeney.

Dark clouds were scudding across the night sky, but a full moon would occasionally peek out from behind the dark masses. It was five minutes to local midnight by Egil's watch.

Almost as if on cue, a long, dark car pulled up on the street in front of the lot. The two elves stepped out from either side. They were dressed in dark business suits, but there was no concealing the abnormally thin figures and the long white hair of their elfin bodies. Egil had halfway expected the pair to come armed with swords, but no such weapons were visible. He did think that he could detect the bulge of shoulder holsters under the tightly cut suit jackets.

The pair of elfin bodyguards gave the empty lot a once over. They were evidently satisfied, as one of them—Egil thought it was Jones—opened the rear door of the car and bent down to speak to the passenger. A moment later Feeney stepped out of the car.

He looked over the lot, and seeing only the leprechaun, Jack, and Egil, he started to walk over. Smith and Jones fell in behind, the two elves towering over their employer. When they had come within ten feet they stopped, the two elves spreading out to either side. Egil noticed that they were looking nervously at Jack and himself—particularly at Jack. This clearly was not what they had expected, and Jack, to those who understood such things, radiated a certain power.

"So, O'Shaunesy, what did you want to talk to me about? Are you ready to sell out?"

"I'll never sell me Pot O'Gold to the loikes of you, Feeney," the leprechaun spat.

"Then why the meeting?" Feeney said uneasily.

"I want you and your pointy-eared minions to leave me and the Pot O' Gold alone," O'Shaunesy replied.

Jones reached into his jacket and his hand came out with an automatic pistol held in his unnaturally long fingers, but Feeney motioned him to stop. He glared at the leprechaun but the pistol dropped to his side.

"You sawed-off little runt," Feeney said. "I've been playing gentle with you so far. But it seems to me I've got all the cards in this game. You better sell me that cheap saloon of yours or else."

"Or else what, rat boy?"

"Or I just might let my friends here have their way with you. I don't think they like leprechauns."

"Are you threatening me?" O'Shaunesy exclaimed waving his walking stick in Feeney's direction.

"Yeah. I'm threatening you. Sell or I'll burn you out."

"That's just what I've been waiting for," O'Shaunesy said.

Suddenly from out of the darkness came a voice, "Charles Feeney. I'm arresting you for extortion." Collins had appeared from behind Feeney with the rest of the policemen. The officers quickly formed a ring around the group.

"You think your gang of two-bit coppers are a match for elves, O'Shaunesy?"

"They are when accompanied by wizards. Fiorordan and Elderasnam, I seize you in the name of the High King of Tara," Egil said, hoping he had got the pronunciation of the two elves true names correctly.

"The High King is long dead, mortal," Fiorordan, aka "Smith," said.

"Brain Boru may be dead, but the terms of the Grand Compact still hold on both sides of the border. Surrender or your lives are forfeit."

"Bold talk, wizard, but can your actions match your words?" He started to bring up the pistol he held in his hand.

Suddenly, the gun began to glow. There was the smell of burning flesh. Both elves gave a cry and tossed their weapons to the ground.

"Thanks, Jack," Egil said.

"Don't mention it, lad." With everyone's attention focused on Egil and O'Shaunesy, the elder wizard had quietly been working a spell. Wielding a silver knife and a rowan branch, he had caused the iron in the elves' pistols to heat up to the burning point with a spell.

"Collins," Egil commanded, "put the handcuffs on these two. The ones of cold forged iron."

"Slap the Darby's on the pointy-eared varmints, Constable," O'Shaunesy chimed in.

Two of the policemen grabbed each of the elves by the arms while a third clicked the specially prepared shackles on their hands and feet.

"They're secured," Collins said. "For the moment."

"We shouldn't have to wait long. I think it's time to open the portal to the half world, Jack."

The wizard set to work. From the ever present carpetbag in which he kept his magical supplies he drew out a bag of chalk dust. Using the rowan branch he drew a pentagram around the group, filling in the lines with the chalk. When the figure was completed he chanted a spell in a language that Egil recognized as an ancient form of Gaelic while he sealed the figure with an elaborate knot of lines drawn with the silver knife.

Feeney he positioned at one point of the pentagram, the two elves occupied the points opposite. O'Shaunesy took the point to his left while Egil took that to his right. Collins and the patrolmen remained outside the figure.

Jack set up a small brazier in the center of the pentagram and started a small fire within. When the flames had died down to coals after a few minutes he produced a packet of herbs and tossed them onto the fire producing a small cloud of not unpleasant smelling smoke, much like that of a fine pipe tobacco.

"If everyone is ready?"

Jack again began to chant in Gaelic, though Egil recognized a few words of Elvish. The two elves were looking decidedly unhappy.

After a few minutes a golden glow began to appear around the pentagram. By some process which Egil didn't pretend to understand a sixth point began to materialize between Jack and himself, the figure rearranging itself to form a six perfect pointed star. As it solidified a figure appeared in the new position.

The new arrival was definitely an elf, but whereas the two in chains were swarthy, untrustworthy looking beings the newcomer was taller and of a fair complexion. His long hair was more silver than white as was the cloak which he wore. The effect was of almost blinding beauty.

"Who summons Ealodrehin, Reeve of Oberon's Court?"

"Jack the Smith," the elder wizard answered.

"It's been a long time Jack," the elf said with a smile. "You look different now. Mortality weighs on you."

"It is human nature, friend."

"Are these the two?" he said looking with disgust on the Swart elves.

"These are the ones. They have broken the Compact."

"And more laws of Faerie than I care to enumerate. Do you surrender them into my custody to treat as Oberon decrees?"

"We do."

"Then I accept them."   With a clap the two elves disappeared.

"Are you satisfied that Oberon has kept his part of the Compact?"

"We are."

"Then our business here is done." The golden elf turned as if to go. "Oh, next time, don't wait so long, Jack. I always found you amusing."   With that the elf and the glow disappeared leaving the pentagram just a chalk figure in the dirt. Jack swiftly erased the remnants with his foot.

"Is that it then?" Liam Collins asked.

"As far as those two go," Egil answered.

"They'll not be back in your lifetime, if ever," Jack affirmed.

"And Feeney?"

"He's yours to deal with, though I'd hurry to catch him."

While the others had been preoccupied with the elf's exit, Feeney had started to slip away. He didn't get far, though, before O'Shaunesy had stuck his walking stick between his legs tripping him up. Kowalski was quick to grab him.

"I think the detective would like to have some words with you, Charlie," Kowalski said as he slapped an ordinary pair of handcuffs on Feeney.

After the detective had called for a patrol car to pick up his prisoner O'Shaunesy said. "I'd loik to thank all you lads proper. If you'll join me back at the Pot O' Gold, the first drink's on me." After a moment the leprechaun added, "Aye, and the second. I'm feelin' in a generous mood after the nights work."

The second drink turned into a third. The patrolmen had gathered around an old piano in the back of the saloon and were singing as many Irish songs as they could remember. It developed that Kowalski had a fine tenor voice.

Jack and Egil had taken a place at the bar and were toasting each other over a glass of Irish. O'Shaunesy had disappeared, but as they sipped their whisky he appeared through the hole leading to the cellar. He was carrying a small leather bag in his hand.

"I'm grateful for all you've done, councilor. Never let it be said that Seamus O'Shaunesy doesn't pay his debts. I'd like you to have this as a show of appreciation," he said as he handed over the bag.

"There are still a few matters outstanding. Like your license and the condemnation proceedings," Egil protested.

"Which I'm sure you will deal with promptly and efficiently, councilor."

"Thank you, then," Egil said opening the bag.   He dumped out the contents into the palm of his hand revealing a dozen large gold coins, coins which must have weighed an ounce each.

"I thought that the story about a pot of gold was just a legend," Egil said.

"Just because a story is folklore doesn't mean it isn't true," the leprechaun said with a wink.   "Can I stand you lads to another round on the house?"

What's This Zombie Doing in My Gumbo?

WHAT'S THIS ZOMBIE DOING IN MY GUMBO?

☆   ☆   ☆   ☆   ☆

Egil Njalsson stared out the dirty window of his office into the evening sky. It had rained earlier and the pavement of the street below shone slick and oily, reflecting the glare of the neon signs in the window of the tattoo parlor across the street. Off in the distance he could still see the occasional flash of lightning from the mid-summer thunderstorm.

Business had been slow lately, as it always seemed to be in July, and at the moment the most pressing concern Egil had was what he was going to do about his dinner. As he weighed his options, a late model sedan pulled up and parked across the street. From the shape of the antenna he recognized it for an unmarked police car, which wasn't surprising considering the neighborhood his law office was in.

His suspicions were confirmed a moment later when a tall, heavily built black man in a worn suit stepped out of the driver's side. Egil recognized him as a detective on the police's serious crimes squad. He'd never had dealings with him; his practice tended toward commercial and patent work, but he had spent enough time around the courthouse to know him by sight.

The detective looked both ways before crossing to the near side of the street. From his vantage point, Egil couldn't see where he was going, but it looked as if he was headed for the entrance of the shabby three story office building where his own two room suite lay. Thoughts of dinner receded in the lawyer's mind.

Of course, the detective might have business with one of the other tenants in the building. There was an accountant, a property management company, even a portrait photographer and a couple of other offices, the nature of whose business remained a mystery to him, but none of those usually worked into the evening. After seven, Egil usually had the building to himself, if one didn't consider the janitor and the cleaning lady who came in once a week to spread the dirt around in the halls. Somehow, he suspected that the detective's business was with him, though for the life of him he couldn't see what it could be. Neither of the briefs he was working on at the moment would seem to have any connection with criminal matters.

He could hear the heavy tread of the detective in the stairwell, the building didn't run to luxuries like an elevator, and then along the hall leading to his office. A large shadow cast by the small bulb in the hall fixture appeared in the frosted glass of the door in the outer room of the suite, followed a moment later by a heavy handed knock.

Egil turned from the window and crossed the suite to the door and turning the dented brass handle opened it.

"Yes, can I help you?" he asked. He found himself looking up at a face of deep brown skin under a shaved head. He remembered hearing that the detective had played defensive end for the university football team and might have had a career in the pros if he hadn't blown out his knee his rookie year. It looked as though despite the knee the detective still kept himself in shape, as there didn't seem to be much fat on his two hundred and eighty pound frame.

"Are you Egil Njalsson, the lawyer?" the detective responded. Egil was coming to hate the sound of that question. It never bode well.

"Yes, I am. What can I do for you, detective? Is this a police matter?"

"No. It's personal," the other answered defensively.

"Why don't you come in then and we can discuss it in the office."

The detective entered, giving the place a professional once over with his eyes. From his expression, it was clear that the opinion he was forming was not high. The furniture was second hand at best and much of it belonged to another decade if not another century. Only their general shabby condition prevented them from being antiques.

Egil took a seat in the chair behind his desk and waved the detective into a chair on the other side that he kept clear for clients.

"Joe O'Neil recommended you. He said you knew about—" there was a hesitation, "things."

That explained it, Egil thought. Joe O'Neil was a beat cop who was also a friend. The "things" the detective mentioned with such trepidation, were magics, and not the modern scientific magics that had brought the world such wonders as etheric communications, lighting elementals, and television, but the nitty-gritty, down-and-dirty dealings with the half world that run just shy of the dark arts. It seemed that Egil was acquiring a reputation, whether deserved or not, for being able to help those who found themselves confronting certain dark powers who best remain unnamed.

Before law school, Egil had received a degree from CalThaum, the best university in the country for the scientific study of the magical arts. Of course, he had received his degree during one of the periodic economic busts and it had seemed like a good idea at the time to find a profession that paid better, like the law. Which was why he eked out a living making patent applications and writing up contracts for the scientists and engineers who had stuck it out and become millionaires by developing the latest spells and potions. Along the way though, he had developed the habit of stumbling into one situation after another involving the dread powers and managed to pick up enough of the kind of knowledge they didn't teach in universities to stay alive while doing it.

"Just how do these 'things' concern you? I'm sorry, I didn't get your name, detective?"

"Robert, Dupree, Detective Sergeant Robert Dupree, though most people call me Bubba. And it's not me that I'm worried about, it's my father."

Egil noted the genuine concern in the detective's voice.

"Why don't you start at the beginning, then, Mr. Dupree?"

"Well, it goes back to New Orleans." He pronounced it as more or less one word. "That's where I'm from originally. I came up north here to play ball at the university. When I injured my knee, I knew I couldn't make it in the pros. I'd gotten my degree in pre-law and police science, so I just kind of fell into being a policeman. They were only too glad to hire an ex-football player, especially if he was black, if you know what I mean. I didn't mind. I got the job and I've been a pretty good cop if I say so myself."

From what Egil had heard, that was true. They hadn't crossed paths professionally but O'Neil had described him as a hard-assed but straight and honest cop. Given the state of the force, that was saying something.

"Anyway, like I said, I'm from New Orleans, and my dad was a chef down there, and a damned good one, too. But after the big hurricane, the city kind of shut down, and he was out of work. So I moved him up here. Well, I had a little money set aside, so I set him up in a little restaurant. Not a big place, but clean and the food is good, Creole, Cajun, catfish, crawdads, po' boys, and gumbo. Things like that. It's been doing pretty good, too, until recently." As the detective spoke, his accent, which had been barely perceptible, became more pronounced.

"What happened then?"

"Well, some other folk moved up from New Orleans, too, folk that didn't like my daddy. I don't know what the original cause was, but it's been going on since before I was born, maybe since before my dad was born. Down in New Orleans, things were kind of kept in check, there were too many parties involved. But up here, the old rules don't seem to apply. Somebody's got it out for my daddy, and they aren't above using some bad stuff to help them."

"By 'bad stuff' I assume you mean magic?"

"Magic, voodoo, I don't know much about that kind of stuff, but that's what they're using."

"Just what kind of things are we talking about?"

"It started small at first. A case of beer going bad, fish spoiling, that kind of thing. Then it started escalating. There was a fire in the kitchen. A dead rat was found during a health department inspection. My daddy's a first class cook. He don't allow no rats. I know that. And all the time these little threats kept appearing. You know, little images with pins stuck in 'em, Hex signs painted on the back door in chicken blood. All kind of nasties."

"Well, my daddy tries to take care of it himself. He's got some tricks of his own, and he didn't want to worry me, but then this last thing happened, and he couldn't keep it from me anymore."

"And what was that?"

"He was charged with turning someone into a zombie. He was arrested and I had to go bail him out. That's when he had to tell me what's been goin' on, and that's when I knew I needed a lawyer, and one who knows about 'things.'"

Egil tried to keep his expression blank, but was having a hard time of it. The other things the detective had described were all small time spells. Illegal, yes, if the intent was to harm, but petty crimes. Turning someone into a zombie was something else, entirely. It wasn't an area of magic that Egil was that familiar with, but it could only be done by invoking the dark powers. It was black magic, pure and simple, and a serious felony. It also wasn't something that the D. A. would file charges on unless there was solid evidence.

"Who is he alleged to have turned into a zombie?"

"There's another restaurant just down the street from my daddy's place. It's run by another guy from New Orleans that came up after the hurricane. Well his cook is the one that's supposed to have been turned into a zombie."

"That's pretty hard to fake. There are tests that can be run."

"Oh, he's a zombie, all right. There ain't no doubt about it. But I'm tellin' you, it wasn't my daddy that did it. He's a good man. He'd never do a thing like that."

"The question is, can we prove it. But before I can do anything, I'd like to talk with your father. Can you arrange a meeting?"

"He's probably still at the restaurant. Are you hungry, Mr. Njalsson?"

Egil thought to himself that at least one of his problems was solved.

☆   ☆   ☆   ☆   ☆

The restaurant turned out to be on a busy commercial street on the east side of the city. Not the best of neighborhoods, but not the worst, either. A block or two off the street was where a lot of students from the university lived, and a few blocks beyond that were some nice older places favored by artists and professors. Much of the rest of the neighborhood was given over to older rental properties where the rent was low, attracting a mix of ethnic groups and the elderly.

The restaurant was located in an old store front. A sign above the door proclaimed it "The New Orleans Café." The inside was about what was to be expected, a dozen or so tables arranged around the long, narrow room with the kitchen at the back. The tables and chairs were an odd assortment that looked as if they had been picked up cheap at second hand sales. Old Mardi Gras posters lined the walls, except where they alternated with photos of a football player, presumably Bubba Dupree. The building showed its age, but the place was scrupulously clean.

At a table in the front corner, a quartet of old men were playing cards and nursing beers. They must have been regulars, because they waved a greeting to the detective as they entered. A couple of the other tables were occupied by what looked like students, but other than that, the place was empty. Of course, it was nearly nine. Egil noted a small shrine to MaMa LuJo in the front window, the sort of thing used to offer protection. Not serious magic, but not entirely innocent, either.

They must have been spotted through the window that led to the kitchen, for before they could sit down a dignified, slender black man of about sixty years of age wearing a white apron came out to greet them. He wasn't short, about Egil's height, but he was at least six inches shorter than the detective.

"You must be Mr. Njalsson, the lawyer," the chef greeted them. "I can see what you're thinking, and yes this boy is my son. His mama was a big woman. Big body and a heart just as big, and I loved every bit of her. Sit yourself down and I'll get you some food, and then we can talk."

The detective pointed to a table next to the kitchen and they sat down. A moment later his father returned with a tray holding three bowls of gumbo and as many bottles of beer. He served them up and then placed the tray on the counter leading to the kitchen before sitting down to join them.

"Eat up, Mr. Njalsson. It ain't fancy, but it's good."

Egil took a spoon of the gumbo. It was good—spicy, but not too hot, and the rice was done just right.

"It's good, Mr. Dupree," he offered.

"Thank you. I want you to know that back in New Orleans I was chef at some of the best French and Creole restaurants in town, but this neighborhood can't afford fancy food, so I cook what they can pay for. Now you finish that up and I'll see what else I got left in the kitchen."

Egil hadn't realized how hungry he was. He finished off the gumbo, sopping the remains up with a thick slice of bread. He saw that the detective had finished before him. His father cleared away the bowls and returned with some plates and two platters, one with pieces of fried catfish and the other with a pile of red beans and rice. "Help yourself," he said. He went back into the kitchen but returned a moment later carrying a folder with some papers in it.

"These are the papers they gave me at the bail hearing," he said.

Egil looked them over as he ate. In addition to the sheet outlining the conditions of bail, there was the charge sheet and the investigating detective's report. The formal charge was "using prohibited magic to harm another individual," a class B felony. About the only thing more serious was rape, kidnapping, or murder. The evidence included a doctor's examination and the report of a forensic magician. He recognized the name of the latter. He was a good man. If he said the victim was a zombie, he was a zombie. The evidence tying Dupree to the crime, though, was mostly circumstantial. That might give him something to work with.

"I have to ask you, Mr. Dupree, did you turn this man into a zombie?"

"I did not," the other replied indignantly. "In the first place, I wouldn't know how. I might know a little ju-ju, a couple of spells and things, but I'm not in that league. That's powerful stuff. And second, I'm not that kind of man."

"Good, Mr. Dupree. I believe you. I just wanted to get that on record. Do you have any idea who might have done it?"

"No, I don't. I wish I did, but I don't."

"What would you do if you did know?" Egil asked.

"Why, I'd tell Bubba here so he could arrest him. That's what I'd do." Egil had no doubt that that was exactly what he would do.

"What about this restaurant that the zombie worked at? You were rivals, weren't you?"

"I didn't think so. They might. People like my food better, and that's a fact. It's cheaper and it tastes better, so I've taken customers away from them, at least before I started having problems. Now, I can believe they might be responsible for some of that stuff. Things like that happened all the time back in New Orleans, little spells and tricks against competitors, not that I ever needed to resort to that. But that's all minor stuff. Not like turning a man into a zombie. That just ain't right."

"So you don't think the owner of this other restaurant might be responsible?"

"I don't see how. He's not that much of a cook, and he sure ain't no great shakes at the other, either."

"Anyone else that's given you problems?"

"No sir, except maybe the Rev. Isaac."

"Rev. Isaac?"

"He runs a little church out of a store front down that way a few blocks. It mostly caters to Haitians and people come up here after the hurricane. He was after me for "contributions" to his church. He said bad things happen to those who oppose God. I sent him packing. From what I've heard, he's not a real Christian minister at all. There's been rumors of strange going's on at that "church" of his after midnight. Me, I've got no fear of the Lord, and I handle charity in my own way."

That seemed to settle that, as far as the detective's father was concerned.

"So, Mr. Njalsson, will you take my father's case?" the detective asked.

"You understand that criminal law is not my specialty. I'm more of a commercial and patent lawyer."

"I know that, Mr. Njalsson. But Bubba says that you know about as much as anyone about the 'other.' As far as I can see, that's what I need, not some shyster who specializes in getting drug dealers and pimps out of jail. I'd be happy if you'd take my case."

"I want to be clear. I haven't had much experience with zombies, either, though I do know someone that probably does."

"I think you know what you need to know," the elder Dupree said.

"If you're agreeable, then, I'll take the case," he held out his hand and the other gave it a firm shake.

"The preliminary hearing is next week. Hopefully I can turn up something by then. Thanks for the dinner. It was some of the best food I've had in quite awhile."

"Thank, You, Mr. Njalsson."

"Well, I've got to get going. I'll be in touch," Egil said as he stood up.

On his way out, one of the card players from the corner table followed him through the door.

"I heard you're going to take Dupree's case. Is that right?" the man said. He looked to be about seventy, dressed in worn but clean clothes.

"Yes, that's right. Why?"

"Well, you just be sure you get him off. Amos is a good man, and he didn't make no zombie. He lets us sit all night without ordering anything but a beer and play cards after the dinner crowd is finished, and then he lets us have anything left over for a quarter a plate." This latter seemed an important point to the old man, making it business, not charity.

"I'll do my best."

"See that you do."

On a hunch, Egil asked, "Do you have any idea who might be behind this zombie business?"

"Can't say for sure, but there's been some strange things going on around here the last few months. People dying that didn't have any business dying. Old folks that no one would miss. You might want to check into that, Mr. Lawyer."

The man seemed completely serious about that. "Thanks for the information. I just might do that. Have a good night."

He left the old man standing in the light from the restaurant's window and headed for his car.

☆   ☆   ☆   ☆   ☆

Egil was definitely feeling out of his depths. His formal training in magic followed the western tradition and was mostly concerned with channeling the forces of nature for useful purposes such as light globes, food preservation spells, and sending communications through the half world, the so called ethernet. It was based on mathematics and a set of rigid principles and laws discovered by centuries of experimentation by the likes of Helmholz and Faraday. Various forms of folk-magic had been covered in a single survey course his sophomore year. Obviously, only the legal forms of magic were taught in universities, and the only time the topic of "black magic" was raised was in the various spells and countermeasures one could take to offer protection. What he did know of Voodoo was that it was a blend of African folk lore and various Christian practices and superstitions, but his practical experience with it was essentially nil.

He knew, however, that there was a vast body of traditional knowledge outside the formal western school, knowledge that dealt with both "white" and "black" magic, as well as "green," "red," and the even more esoteric "blue" magic. Various events in his law practice had brought him into contact with some of this knowledge, and while he was by no means an expert, his horizons had expanded considerably since he had graduated from Cal Thaum.

Fortunately, he had one resource which he could turn to when confronted with subjects outside his expertise, a former client who had become both a friend and a mentor, a self-professed hedge wizard who just might conceivably be the most powerful magician alive. Or not. It was always hard to tell with Jack.

A run-down second-hand store would hardly seem likely to be the residence and business place of such a powerful wizard, but, in fact, that was where Jack had lived as long as Egil had known him. He headed there after leaving the restaurant, stopping at a convenience store for a suitable offering.

The lights were off in the store when he pulled up, but somewhat to his surprise, the front door was unlocked. He entered cautiously, not so much for fear of what he might find, but more to avoid tripping over the odd jumble of old furniture and junk that crammed the storefront.

"Jack? Are you home?" he called out.

From the back room came a response, "I'll be with you in a moment, Egil." Shortly thereafter a middle aged Hispanic woman came hurriedly out of the backroom clutching a small brown bottle in her hands. She left through the front door without a word.

The curtain covering the doorway to the back parted revealing the shadow of a wiry man of middle height.

"Sorry about that. Just a bit of business. A marital aid. Come on in," the form in the doorway said. It was never clear to Egil if Jack ever sold any of the bric-a-brac in the shop. He knew that the majority of his income came from telling fortunes and selling potions and amulets. None of this was strictly legal, but as none of his customers ever filed complaints, Jack operated under the radar of authority.

"Ah, I see you've brought some refreshments. Have you eaten?"

"As a matter of fact I have. But don't let that stop you."

"No, I'm fine. Sit down. Just let me get some glasses." He retired up a narrow set of stairs in the back that led to the living quarters above.

The backroom that Egil found himself in was Jack's office, study, and library. In contrast to the front of the shop it was scrupulously neat. A small, green baize covered table occupied the center of the room with a chair on each side. In the middle of the table under a black velvet cloth was, Egil knew, a crystal ball. Whether it was functional or window-dressing, he wasn't sure as Jack had never had recourse to use it in his presence.

Two walls of the chamber were covered with bookshelves, the contents of which had always been a source of amazement to the lawyer. Along with the latest technical volumes on various branches of magic, science, and mathematics were older volumes in a variety of languages, some of which Egil couldn't even recognize. One section contained volumes of manuscripts some dating back centuries. From previous perusals, he knew that some of them were not even supposed to exist anymore. Many a university library would have paid any price for half of the collection.

The blank spots on the walls not covered by bookcases contained a collection of old photographs, mostly of groups of carefully posed men standing self-consciously for the camera. The collection would have been an ethnographer's dream, as the groups captured in the photos included Tibetan monks, Native American shamans, gypsies, Indian fakirs, students at a rabbinical college, and at least one that seemed to be posed before a cathedral in Cambridge. The curious feature was that in each of the photos there was one figure that, despite race and location, bore an uncanny resemblance to Jack, which considering that some of the photos had to be nearly a century and a half old was definitely odd. Jack had never given his age, and by now Egil was afraid to ask for fear of what the answer would be.

Jack returned from the kitchen upstairs with two beer glasses, and setting out coasters, placed them on the green baize of the table. During the last month or so, Jack had been living in the guise of a Irish gypsy, so Egil had bought a six pack of cold Smithwick's at the store. The old wizard had the habit of changing his persona frequently, which made keeping up with his tastes a challenge. His brief period as a Tibetan monk a few months ago had proved to be a real trial. Fortunately no real crisis had come up during that period as finding fermented yak milk is never easy.

"So what brings you out at this hour, lad. Vampires? Werewolves?"

"Voodoo, or more particularly, zombies."

"Zombies? What have you gotten yourself into?" Jack asked.

Egil gave a brief outline of the situation.

"Interesting. The subject of Voodoo is really more one of religion than magic. Most of the rituals and practices are relatively harmless and more in the nature of propitiatory rites rather than true magic. The roots of Voodoo can be traced to African animist religions on which a thin veneer of Christianity has been overlaid. Not that there isn't a certain amount of power in such things, but it lies with asking the intercession of various saints and gods rather than an appeal to the dark powers. This is particularly true in and around New Orleans as opposed to how things are done in Haiti.

"Zombies are something of a completely different nature. There are some authorities that claim that the process isn't even really magical, but instead involves the use of certain drugs derived from the puffer fish and a fair dose of psychological conditioning. Of course, needless to say, very little research has been done in the area."

The fact that Jack had gone into lecture mode didn't strike Egil as at all unusual. He frequently did so when discussing esoteric topics. He suspected that at least one point in time his friend had been part of a university faculty. He had once shown Egil a diploma from the Sorbonne for one Jacques Krieger, though of course the date on the certificate would seem to make it impossible that Krieger and Jack were one and the same person.

"Of course, there are competing theories including some that require the direct involvement of demons or other dark powers. I tend to have an open mind on this one. I'm afraid this is one area where my experience is limited. How certain are you that the man is really a zombie?"

"Well, there seems little doubt that the victim has been turned into a zombie, by whatever means. I know the forensic magician who did the evaluation by reputation. He's no fool, and he's much too careful to state something in a report if he isn't completely sure of his facts. If I'm to mount a defense I need to prove that either someone else is responsible or that there is no way my client could be responsible. Unfortunately, he seems to be a practitioner of at least some minor aspects of Voodoo, namely protective spells and amulets."

"Ah, yes. Gris-gris. Not at all unusual for someone of his background."

"That's all very well, but it may be enough to convict him in the eyes of a northern jury. They tend to take a rather dim view of this sort of thing."

"I see your point. The problem is, without direct contact, I'm not sure I can tell you anything helpful. Is there any way that I could see the victim in person?"

"I'm not sure how. If you had some professional standing, I might be able to get access as an expert witness. But I doubt that I could get a judge to agree to allow an antiques dealer interview the victim."

Jack thought this over for a bit. "What about a professor of psychology, say someone who has written some papers on the fugue state?"

"That might be allowable."

"Give me a minute," Jack said, getting up and going over to an old roll-top desk against the wall. He rummaged around for a bit and then came up with some papers.

"Would Professor Jakob Svaboda do?" he said handing Egil the papers.

One proved to be an expired Czech passport with Jack's photo, while the other was a diploma from the University of Vienna dated 1932 awarding a doctorate to one Jakob Svaboda.

"This is supposed to be you?" Egil asked skeptically.

"That surprises you? Of course the good professor is retired now, but I believe he is still listed as an emeritus member of the faculty in Prague. He wrote some interesting papers. You should read them sometime."

"This might get you in if I wave them in front of the judge without letting him look at the dates too closely. I'll see what I can arrange."

"I'm afraid there's not much else I can do until then. I will keep my ear open for any gossip, though. Do you want another beer?"

"No," Egil said. "It's getting late and I have plenty of work to do tomorrow."

Egil spent much of the next day working on the case. The biggest problem proved to be getting permission for his expert witness, Jack, to examine the victim. The D. A. only caved in when he threatened to get a court order from a judge. His office was already under pressure about claims that it had suppressed evidence in several high profile cases the previous year. Egil was learning to play the game, and his threat brought a sudden wave of cooperation from the prosecutor. Not only was access to the victim to be granted the nest day, but a copy of the complete evidence file on the case would be sent over to his office by messenger. All this helpfulness made Egil wonder if there wasn't something more behind the case than a rivalry between two restaurants that had gotten out of hand.

The file, when he examined it, proved less than helpful. From the forensic evidence, there was little doubt that the victim, one William Johnston, former chef at "Francois's Café", was a zombie. Egil knew by reputation that the forensic magician was a thorough and competent investigator, and his report gave him no reason to change the opinion. He had run all the conventional tests and a few others that caused Egil to lift his eyebrow. The attending physician's report concurred with the diagnosis. Johnston was definitely a zombie.

The evidence linking Amos Dupree to the case was a lot more circumstantial, though. There was a statement by the owner of "Francois's," Antoine Francois, that there was bad blood between the two, that mutual threats had been made, and that certain incidents of a magical nature had occurred at his restaurant which he attributed to Dupree's actions. Several witnesses corroborated Francois's story, though no actual proof was given. Several fetishes had been found at the café which were now in the evidence locker.

The investigating detectives had interviewed Dupree. Their report noted the presence of the Mama Lujo shrine in the accused's restaurant, and his supposed familiarity with Voodoo. However, neither of the detectives had any training or knowledge in magic. A forensic team had visited the restaurant and noted the presence of certain spices and herbs, some of which were used in the ceremonies involved with Voodoo and zombie rituals. This was not surprising as they were also common ingredients in Creole and Haitian cooking.

The most damaging evidence was a statement from one Rev. Isaac, who ran a church in the neighborhood. He stated that the victim helped out with food preparation at a kitchen he ran to feed in his words "the poor and unfortunate." The evening before he became a zombie, he had seemed nervous and unsettled. When the reverend inquired as to the cause, the victim was frightened by Amos Dupree, and that the latter had threatened him with dire consequences in retaliation for acts against his restaurant. The victim had also stated that he had had nothing to do with those acts. He had gone on to state of Amos Dupree that it had been well known back in New Orleans that he was a Voodoo practitioner of some power and had been responsible for "bad things" happening to those that crossed him. Rev. Isaac had counseled forgiveness and urged the victim to try to make things up with Dupree and had offered his good offices to this end, but when he had approached Dupree the latter had ordered him out of his establishment.

This statement had formed the foundation on which the D. A. had built his case for charging Dupree. The Rev. Isaac, though unconventional, seemed to be a prominent figure in the community and was well known for his charitable works, in particular running a soup kitchen that catered to the poor, elderly, and homeless.

It seemed to Egil, that without the statement of Rev. Isaac, the case would fall apart, but there seemed no clear way to attack it.

☆　　☆　　☆　　☆　　☆

By the time that he had sifted his way through the evidence report it was well after noon and Egil felt the need for sustenance. He thought for a moment of returning to

Dupree's café, but as that would involve a drive across town, he decided on a quick burger instead.

The best burgers within walking distance were at an all night dinner near the police department. As it was also close to the court house, Egil had stumbled onto it early in his career as a lawyer, as the food was both plentiful and cheap. Not surprisingly, these qualities also appealed to cops going on or off shift, and the place was a regular hangout for the boys and girls in blue. It was at that diner that Egil had made the acquaintance of Joe O'Neil, who had played a role in various of his more unusual cases.

However, he was somewhat surprised to meet him there on this occasion as he was currently assigned to the graveyard shift and was not scheduled for duty for another nine hours.

"Join me, councilor?" the Irishman asked, indicating the stool next to him at the counter.

"Don't mind if I do," Egil replied with a grin. "What are you doing here at this hour? I thought you were working the late shift."

"I am, but this homeless case has got us working extra duty."

"Homeless case? I must be out of touch," Egil responded.

"Well, they're trying to keep it hush-hush, if you know what I mean. They don't want to start a panic."

"Sounds intriguing. What gives?"

"Well, if you ask me, it's nothing. But there have been a number of homeless men that have been found dead over on the east side. Nothing suspicious about the deaths, mind you.   They all seem to have died of 'natural causes.' Still, there's been more than a dozen of them in the last two months. Usually there'd only be one or two in that period."

While Joe was talking, the waitress came over. He ordered a cheeseburger with Swiss and a slice of raw onion with fries and a cup of coffee. After she had left Egil said, "That's interesting. I was talking to a man in that neighborhood who mentioned that some strange things have been going on. People dying."

"Yeah, it's got people kind of nervous. There's a lot of old folks in that area, and it's getting so they're afraid to go out after dark. That's why they're trying to keep things quiet."

"They don't seem to be doing too good a job of it."

"Do they ever?" O'Neil commented.

The waitress brought his coffee. As usual, it wasn't great java, but it was strong.

"Say, did Bubba Dupree ever get in touch with you? Seems his old man has got himself in a jam of some sort."

"Yeah, he did. I'm working on it now. You don't know anything about the case, do you?"

"No, can't say I do. I didn't work it, and I've been too busy doing double shifts to catch any rumors. Something about zombies, isn't it?"

"Yeah. At least one. Dupree's been accused of turning a rival chef into one."

"Think he did it? Bubba Dupree's a hard-ass, but he's a good cop, if you know what I mean."

"No. I'm pretty sure he's innocent. All I have to do is prove it."

The waitress dropped off his burger and fries. Egil spread some ketchup on it and took a bite.

"If there's anything I can do, let me know. Well, I've got to report for roll call. The wife isn't crazy about these double shifts, I can tell you."

"Take care."

The big cop got up and left. Egil noticed that he had left the bill lying on the counter. He covered it with a ten and had a fry.

☆   ☆   ☆   ☆   ☆

Jack was waiting when Egil picked him up for the examination of the zombie. Uncharacteristically, he was wearing a suit that was of undeniable high quality if several decades out of date. Egil hoped it would only make him look more like a European scholar.

Johnston was being held in protective custody in the psych ward at the university's hospital. There were the usual delays, examination of credentials and permission from the D.A., but after a half hour they were passed through a locked security door and escorted to a small interview room.

The zombie was sitting motionless in a straight backed chair. Johnston was a black man, about fifty years of age, and physically seemed to be in reasonably good shape except for a slight lack of muscle tone that could be attributed to his being a zombie. There was a complete lack of expression to his face, and the eyes that looked out in an unfocused gaze looked empty and soulless.

Jack had traded the carpetbag in which he usually carried his magical apparatus for a more conventional Gladstone. He opened this, and drawing out a small flashlight and a reflex hammer began to examine Johnston in what, Egil had to admit, was an apparently professional manner. Not that he doubted his friend's competency, especially when it came to the magical, but he did have a tendency for the unorthodox.

After using the flashlight to check eye dilation, he applied the hammer to various parts of the zombie's anatomy. This was followed up by a small pin which Jack used to test several places on the hands and neck.

"Well?" Egil asked.

"He's a zombie. What did you expect?"

"I don't know. You were the one who wanted this examination."

"Patience, Egil. I just wanted to make sure that what we are dealing with is a genuine zombie and not some other sort of drug or trauma induced state. Now that we have established that fact we can proceed accordingly."

As always, though it never ceased to surprise Egil, Jack had completely immersed himself in his new persona as an "expert." He was acting, speaking, and even thinking like a doctor. Egil found it disconcerting.

"Just what does that mean."

"We know he is a zombie. The questions at hand are 'How he became one?' and 'Who is responsible?'"

"And you can determine that?"

"Possibly. I won't know until I've run a few tests."

If anyone was listening in, Egil thought, they would be reassured by the last statement. What could be more medical?

Jack produced a small vial from his bag and using a tiny silver knife drew a few drops of blood from the zombie's left thumb. To this he added a small bit of powder that he flicked from a little cloth bag, reciting in what Egil took to be some form of Creole French. Suddenly, the blood, which had been deep crimson, turned a positively bilious yellow.

"Ah, ha," Jack said.

"Ah, ha?" Egil asked. He had no idea what his friend had just done. It wasn't the sort of thing they had covered at CalThaum.

"I've detected a trace of the toxin of the puffer fish."

"Which means what?"

"That the ritual used to induce the zombie state included the administration of the toxin of that fish."

"Wouldn't any toxin have been eliminated from the body already? He's been here in the hospital almost two weeks."

"Oh, the actual toxin was probably eliminated in a day or two after the ceremony. What this test detects is the presence of the essence of the toxin. That will remain as long as he's a zombie. But I'm not surprised that the forensic magic specialist missed it. This test is somewhat esoteric and not really legally approved."

"So what does it mean?"

"It means that whoever did this is the real deal. This isn't just a case of a little psychological hocus pocus or brainwashing or something of that nature. This is magic of the highest and darkest order. It also points to someone with a Haitian background rather than someone from New Orleans."

"Would Mr. Dupree have the knowledge to perform the ceremony?"

"I would sincerely doubt it. After our meeting I went to his restaurant without mentioning our connection. By the way, I had a very good Jambalaya while I was there. He really is a good cook. I wanted to see if I could detect anything of a magical essence about him. What there was, was of minor strength and completely benign in nature. Anyone who could perform the zombie ritual in this case would exude power in his aura."

"OK. Can we prove it, though? In a court of law."

"That's the next step. While I was at the restaurant, I took some samples from Amos Dupree. I can use those to run a test against samples from Johnston, here. If Dupree was responsible there should be a positive reaction. You should know the method—Helmholz's Congruence."

Egil didn't want to know how Jack had obtained his "samples." Helmholz's Congruence, however, was something that he did know. It was a basic test involving the Law of Sympathy. He had learned to perform it in the lab course for Alchemy 1a his freshman year at CalThaum.

Jack produced another test tube from his bag. This one was stoppered and contained what looked like several hairs, presumably from Amos Dupree. With a small scissors, this time of plain stainless steel, Jack cut a few hairs from Johnston's head and placed them in the test tube. To this he added a clear liquid which he poured from a small reagent bottle. He replaced the stopper and shook the tube vigorously.

Nothing happened.

"Nothing happened," Egil stated.

"Exactly. This is what one would expect if Amos Dupree was not responsible for turning Mr. Johnston into a zombie. In fact, it proves that Amos Dupree has never performed an act of magic with Johnston as the object. Ipso Facto as you lawyers like to say, your client is innocent."

"Will this stand up in court?" Egil asked. Without consulting case law, he wasn't sure, though somehow he felt that Jack was.

"I suggest you ask the forensic magician on the case to perform the test himself, and to do so before the initial hearing."

"That should be easy enough to do. But if Dupree didn't make Johnston a zombie, then who did?"

"That I can't tell at this time, lad. What I can tell you is that he is probably Haitian and that he is channeling some very dark powers. I'd be on my guard, or you might end up like our friend here."

☆   ☆   ☆   ☆   ☆

The preliminary hearing was held several days later. Normally, such hearings are brief affairs where the prosecution presented evidence that a crime has been committed and that there were sufficient grounds to bring the accused to trial. The defense had the opportunity to counter these grounds, but unless they could prove a very strong case for dismissal, the case would be scheduled for trial.

The judge hearing the case was William Solomon. Egil was somewhat surprised, as he was the most senior district judge and usually was dealt the most important cases. He wondered whether there was some political maneuvering going on behind the scenes. The good news was that Solomon had a reputation for both honesty and fairness.

The prosecuting attorney was Walker, a ferret-faced little weasel with a perpetual five o-clock shadow and narrow beady eyes. The rumor was that he had political ambitions far above the district attorney's office, and he had a reputation for grandstanding in court in high profile cases.

Egil took his place at the defendant's table next to Amos Dupree. The old man smiled, but looked nervous. His son, Bubba, was in the gallery. Egil had thought it best not to bring Jack into court as his credentials were somewhat dubious. Hopefully his testimony wouldn't be needed.

The bailiff entered the courtroom and announced, "All rise. District Court Number Seven is now in session, Judge William Solomon presiding."

The judge took his seat behind the bench and announced, "Counselors, this is a preliminary hearing. Let's try to make it as brief and businesslike as possible. I have other cases pending today. If the case goes to trial you will each have plenty of opportunities to make speeches."

The first witness called was the responding officer. The gist of his testimony was that an employee of the restaurant had come into work one morning and found the chef in a catatonic state. He had called emergency services. An ambulance had been dispatched along with a police squad. From comments made by the restaurant works, it was suspected that magic might be involved. The victim had been taken to the university hospital.

The second witness was the doctor who had made the preliminary examination at admittance. He gave a statement identifying the victim as a black male, age fifty-one named William Johnston and employed as a chef. He was awake but unresponsive. Since admittance his condition had not changed. For neither of these witnesses had Egil posed any questions.

The third witness was where it was going to get interesting. This was Dr. Jervis, the forensic magic specialist. He had a formidable professional reputation and frequently lectured on magical jurisprudence at the university.

After Jervis had stated his position and credentials, the prosecutor asked, "Dr. Jervis, you examined Mr. Johnston. Can you tell us, briefly what you discovered?"

"Mr. Johnston was, as has been described, awake but unresponsive. That is, his eyes were open but he did not react to any external stimuli. There is a fairly standard protocol in cases like these which I followed. Now, there are a number of natural causes of a medical nature that can cause these, but it had been suggested that magic had been involved. I therefore made a number of tests to determine if this was the case."

"And was it?"

"Yes. Magic had definitely been used against Mr. Johnston. I then undertook a more thorough examination with this in mind."

"And what is your conclusion?"

"The indications are that certain rituals common to Haiti had been employed, probably in conjunction with the toxin derived from a puffer fish. In layman's terms, he had been turned into a zombie."

"Thank you, Dr. Jervis. I have no further questions, your honor."

"Does the counsel for the defense have any questions?" the judge asked assuming that there would be none.

"Just a few, your honor."

"Are you challenging the witnesses conclusions or his credentials?"

"No your honor, I fully accept that Mr. Johnston is a zombie, and I have the greatest respect for Dr. Jervis's qualifications and experience, but there are a few points I would like to clarify if I may."

"Very well, but please be brief. You will have your chance if the case comes to trial."

"Yes, your honor. Dr. Jervis. Are you familiar with Helmholz's Congruence?"

"Of course, it is a very basic procedure in forensic magic."

"Could you briefly explain its nature?"

"Any magical act leaves a signature, a magical fingerprint if you will. The procedure called Helmholz's Congruence allows one to establish if a given person is responsible for a particular act. It relies on the Law of Sympathy, one of the fundamental principles of modern magic. It's use in law was established brilliantly by that famous British expert in magical jurisprudence, Dr. John Thorndyke, in 1905 in the case of the Crown vs. Hornby, in which it was proved that a fingerprint used as evidence in the Crown's case had been planted using magical means by someone other than the defendant."

"Objection," the prosecutor shouted. "British case law has no bearing in an American court."

The judge said dryly, "I don't believe that the witness has made a claim to which you can object, Mr. Walker. He has merely stated a historical fact. Continue, Dr. Jervis, but please be brief."

"The test was recognized in the case of the State of Illinois vs. Simpson in 1912 and upheld by the United States Supreme Court the following year. It is today a very common test in forensic magic."

"Thank you, Dr. Jervis. Your point to this is, Mr. Njalsson?" the judge asked.

"Did you, Dr. Jervis, perform this test with the accused Amos Dupree in relation to William Johnston?"

"I did."

"And your conclusion was?"

"That Amos Dupree could not be responsible for turning Mr. Johnston into a zombie, or for performing any other act of magic against him."

"Your honor, in light of this testimony, I would like to move that the case against Amos Dupree be dropped."

"Will the counsels approach the bench?"

"Mr. Walker, why wasn't I made aware that such a test had been made?"

"I was not aware of the fact, myself, your honor."

"I see. Dr. Jervis, I do not believe that this test was mentioned in your report."

"It was not, your honor. I had not made the test at that time. I had examined Mr. Johnston to determine the nature and cause of his condition. At that time, no mention was made of the fact that the police or the prosecutor's office had a suspect in mind, nor had that fact been made known to me subsequently."

"Why then, did you conduct this test."

"It was at the suggestion of the defendant's counsel."

"Ah. And I assume that you had a reason for this suggestion, Mr. Njalsson?"

"As I believed my client to be innocent, it seemed a natural step to take. I was as surprised as you were, your honor, that the test had not been made already. As the witness has stated, the test is a very common one."

"Can you explain this, Mr. Walker?"

"My office assumed that we had sufficient evidence to try the case without it your honor. I am not an expert in forensic jurisprudence."

"Perhaps you should study up on the subject before wasting the court's time again, Mr. Walker. Counsels may withdraw from the bench."

"In light of this new evidence, I grant the defense's motion and dismiss the case. The Court is adjourned."

☆ ☆ ☆ ☆ ☆

They gathered that evening at the New Orleans Café to celebrate, Amos and Bubba Dupree, Jack and Egil. The dinner was decidedly off menu, more French than Creole or Cajun, an example of the type of cooking Amos had done in new Orleans before the hurricane. As they passed the remains of the second bottle of wine around the table, the detective raised his glass.

"I propose a toast. To Egil Njalsson. Thank you for clearing my father's name."

"I would say it was nothing," Egil responded, "but the fact is, the dismissal owes more to Jack than to myself. Once he supplied the evidence establishing that Amos could not be responsible, the rest was easy."

"Then, thanks to you, Jack."

The latter bowed in the detective's direction. "As Egil said, it was no great thing. I merely pointed the forensic magician in the right direction, though I am glad I could be of some small help."

"Whatever the case, I want to thank both of you," Amos then spoke up. "It's a terrible thing being accused of such a crime. We might have had our differences, but I still can't help thinking about that poor man. What do you think will become of him? Will he remain a zombie?"

"That's a good question," Egil answered. "As far as I know, his condition remains the same. Do you have any ideas, Jack?"

"This is a dark part of the lore which thankfully I am not that familiar with. The spell that was involved was a powerful one, and I believe more than human forces are involved. From what I understand of the matter, Johnston will remain a zombie until he dies unless the person responsible is destroyed and the powers behind him are vanished from this world."

"Has there been any progress on that front?" Egil asked.

Bubba Dupree responded, "It's being looked into, but so far no leads have turned up. Right now the department has a more pressing problem that's taking up resources."

"What is that?" Egil asked, "if you can tell us."

The detective sighed and took a sip of his wine.

"The department is trying to keep it quiet," he said after a moment, "but there have been far too many people dying in this neighborhood. At first it just looked like they were dying of natural causes. Most of them were old, living alone, and not in good health. No one suspected anything, so there wasn't any investigation. No autopsies were carried out. But there's been too many to ignore. For the last one that was reported, they called in Dr. Jervis. He found something out about the deaths that has him spooked. Now we've got at least a dozen deaths that have been classified as homicide by magic. There's a full-court press by the department trying to find out what all these old men had in common before word leaks out to the press. Not much effort is being spent on the Johnston case."

"Do you think there might be some kind of connection?"

"I don't know. I wish I did," the detective said. He sounded worried.

"I think, Mr. Dupree," Jack said quietly, "that you should be careful. Someone tried to get at you using this zombie. They're still out there, and they might strike again."

A short time later after that somber note, the dinner party broke up.

☆   ☆   ☆   ☆   ☆

Egil was working in his office a couple of days later when he heard a knock on his door. When he went to answer it he found the hulking form of Bubba Dupree.

"What can I do for you, Detective? Is your father alright?"

"He's ok, but I'm worried about him. He's going along like nothing has happened. I tried to talk him into shutting the restaurant for a few weeks and getting out of town, but he refused. Said he's got people depending on him and he wasn't going to run from any zombie making Loa."

"Just what do you want me to do? Go talk to him?"

"I'm out of my depth, Mr. Njalsson. I'm a cop and an ex-football player. I could protect my father from thugs or ordinary criminals. But I don't know anything about magic or voodoo or anything like that. From what I've heard, you do. Isn't there some kind of mojo or spell or something that you could work to protect him?"

"There are spells of protection, steps that can be taken. I have some knowledge of these things, but I'm a lawyer these days. I'll do what I can of course—"

"What about your friend? Jack? It seemed that he had a lot better idea of what was going on than anyone else. I'd be willing to pay him."

"Yes, Jack might be better equipped for this kind of thing than I am. I'll talk to him. I know he likes your father. How about if I show up at the restaurant around closing. I'll see if I can get Jack, and even if he isn't available, I can put up some protections of my own."

"I'd really appreciate that. I'll let my father know you're coming."

☆　　☆　　☆　　☆　　☆

Jack was available, and when Egil picked him up at his shop around eight he noted that he was carrying the old carpetbag he usually carried on "cases". Egil's own slightly smaller bag was resting on the back seat.

The four old men were in the corner again playing cards when they arrived at the restaurant. The man that had talked to Egil before looked them over and there was hushed comments exchanged between the players. Amos greeted them nervously from behind the counter.

"Bubba said you'd be coming. Don't know what you can do, but folks gettin' kind of nervous. Word's been gettin' out that people been dyin'."

"We'll try to do what we can, Mr. Dupree," Egil said trying to sound reassuring.

"I've tried to do what I can. I got the shrine to Mama Lujo, and I put some hex signs on the back door, but I'm no voodoo priest. That's mostly just tradition and 'atmosphere' as they say."

"We're planning on something a little stronger, I think."

Jack had placed his bag on a chair next to one of the tables and was pulling out various apparatus and placing them on the tables. From a professional standpoint, Egil always found it fascinating watching his friend work. He could understand much of it, but Jack had knowledge of things they had never taught at CalThaum.

"The doors will be the weak points."

"There's just the front and the back, the one in the kitchen. There's a couple of windows in back, too."

"I'll seal those first, then."

He grabbed a black candle, a length of string, and a small silver knife from the items on the table. In the back there were two windows, one above the sink and the other on the far side of a central door above a prep table. The kitchen was, as most small restaurant kitchens are, small and cramped, though arranged neatly. Jack closed the windows tightly and fastened the latches. Taking the string, he cut two equal lengths with the arthame or silver knife. He carefully wrapped the string around the latch, binding the two parts of the window together, and then tying it off with an elaborate knot. He lit the candle from one of the kitchen burners and dripped its molten wax over the knot so that it was completely enclosed in a black ball of wax. Then, taking the knife he carved a strange character into the solidifying surface while chanting a spell. Egil couldn't understand the language, but thought it was Sanskrit. Satisfied, Jack repeated the performance on the other window. During the whole ritual Amos had looked on in amazement.

"Don't, under any circumstances, break that knot or open the window without my permission. The door, I assume, you will need to use."

"Yeah. That opens onto the alley. That's where I bring in all my supplies."

"Too bad."

Jack went out into the front room and returned with a fresh set of articles. He began drawing characters along the door jamb. Taking a stool, he stood on it and continued his drawing on the lintel. This time the characters were in Tibetan. As he worked on the spell Jack recited a chant in that curious voice called "throat-singing" by which Tibetan monks sing two notes at once. Egil's knowledge of Tibetan magical practices was slight, but he could feel the level of power rising in the room.

At the base of the door Jack continued the characters from the frame and drew them out into a mandala on the floor. He finished off the spell with another mandala on the surface of the door."

Stepping back he studied his artwork. He looked satisfied.

"This is a trap. If something gets caught in it, call me. If you need to use the door, you must repeat the password before opening it."

"What's the password?"

"Open Sesame. I thought that was a nice touch," Jack said with a smile. "Now for the front."

By this time, everyone in the place—the four card players, Amos, his kitchen assistant, and Egil—had gathered around to watch.

There was a small shelf in front of each of the large windows that flanked the front door. The shrine to Mama Lujo sat on the one to the left. Jack stood before the shrine and made a little half bow. He then poured a small amount of green liquid from a small bottle at the base of the shrine.

"Absinthe. It can't hurt," he said with a shrug.

He traced a seven pointed pentacle on the shelf next to the shrine, placing characters, this time in archaic Hebrew, at each vertex. For the other window he had a different treatment. From his bag he pulled a large skull. Egil wasn't sure what animal it was, but it had three horns, one over each ear hole and one above the nose. On the shelf he started to make a sand painting using different colored sands. Egil thought he recognized the tradition as Navaho. At this point, Egil wasn't sure if Jack was drawing on so many disparate cultures so as to confuse any enemy, or whether he was just showing off.

He finished off the performance on the door with a curse in Norse runes, smiling at Egil when he had finished. Jack knew Egil's predilection for his Scandinavian ancestors.

Satisfied, Jack sat down in the chair next to his bag.

"Well, that should keep most wizards and small demons at bay at least. But before I get on with the serious work, I think I need a beer." Amos nodded to his assistant who fetched some bottles from the cooler.

Jack drank his beer in silence, though the beverage seemed to restore him. None of the others said anything either, though whether from fear or respect it was hard to say. Finally, after draining the last dregs of the bottle the wizard said, "So much for the preliminaries. It's time to get down to serious work. But for that, everyone but Egil will have to leave. What I am going to do is much too dangerous for the uninitiated."

Egil raised his eyebrow. He had no idea what the elder wizard had planned. Even some of the spells performed so far had been beyond his experience.

The others didn't raise any objections. Despite the intrusion of magic into everyday life, the average layman is mostly oblivious to all but the surface manifestations of the art and woefully ignorant of the forces behind the art. What they had been exposed to tonight would stay with them for a lifetime. One by one they filed out the door.

"Now what?" Egil asked, once the last of them had departed.

"So far, what I have done are protection spells. They are good enough to deter or trap minor spirits or demons and ward off malign influences. But I have a feeling that we are dealing with a darker and more powerful foe, one that will not be stopped by such simple measures. For that, I am going to try something that I have only done three times in my life."

"I'm warning you, it is not without danger. I will be invoking magic that is neither white nor black, but somewhere in between, something gray from the heart of the half world.. You do not have to stay, lad."

Ordinary magic, the commercial stuff of everyday life, was by its very nature and by law white magic, or perhaps green. That was the magic Egil had learned at Cal Thaum. Black magic, the summoning and controlling of demons, was both illegal and damning to its practitioners and studies of it were limited to those steps necessary to counter it. But gray magic was something else, entirely, an unseen force whose very existence had not even been suspected when Egil had been at the university. Only recently had the theories of science even hinted at the possibility of such forces. Yet it didn't surprise Egil that the elder wizard should possess knowledge beyond what was taught in the best schools in the world.

"I'll stay. What do you want me to do?"

"Follow my instruction exactly. And no questions until later. What we are going to try to establish is a center that will actively repel malign forces; deflect them into the unseen dimensions of the half-world in such a way that they may not return."

Egil sensed that the word "may" was being used in the sense that they would not have permission to return rather than the sense that it was possible they might not. In magic, as in so much, the meaning of words has power.

There is little purpose in describing what followed. Ordinary language lacks a reference which would be understandable. At dawn, the two wizards left the café, their object achieved.

☆   ☆   ☆   ☆   ☆

A week passed, then two. Amos had had no more trouble at his café. Whoever, or whatever, had been trying to harm him had decided for the moment to leave him alone. The rest of the community, however, was not so lucky. A dozen more individuals, mostly poor, old men, had been found dead from causes unknown. Something akin to panic was gripping the neighborhood, while the police redoubled their efforts to uncover a link with little to show for it.

For that reason, Egil was not surprised when he received a phone call one night from Bubba Dupree.

"Mr. Njalsson, I need your help," the detective said over the phone. There was noise in the background, the sound of men moving about purposefully.

"Is it your father?" Egil asked.

"No, he's fine. But I'm at my wits end, and I didn't know who else to turn to. Like nearly every other detective in this town, I've been investigating these deaths that have been happening, and I got to tell you, we haven't been getting anywhere. Well, tonight, we found another one, fresh. Except this one I know. He's one of the old men that show up at the café late at night for the leftovers. He may might have been old and he might have been poor, but I would have sworn that he was in pretty good health for all of that. I just don't buy that he died of no natural causes, which is what the M.E. is going to tell me. I was wondering if you and maybe your friend could take a look at the body before we move it."

"Don't take this the wrong way, but I don't want to get on the wrong side of the M.E.'s office by interfering with an official investigation," Egil said. "I do have my law license to consider."

"Don't worry about that," Bubba Dupree said. "I've cleared it with the M.E. He's at as much of a loss as I am."

"If he doesn't object, I can be there in a half hour or so. I'll pick up Jack on the way if he's available."

"I'll be expectin' you," the detective said, and then gave directions. Egil had noticed that the detective had a tendency to lapse into the dialect of his youth when worried. Judging by his speech patterns tonight, he was really concerned.

The body had been discovered in a rooming house that catered to older single men a few blocks south of Dupree's café. Jack had been more than willing to come along, and had only paused long enough to pack his wizard's carpet bag.

There was a squad car with flashing lights on in the street out front as well as a van from the M.E.'s office. The uniformed officer on guard must have been alerted to their coming as he waved them on up the front steps of the building. Bubba Dupree was standing on the second floor landing of the steps in conference with a man wearing a white coverall with "M.E." on the back. When he saw them, he waved them up the steps and made introductions.

"I know this is irregular," the M.E. said, "but at this point I'm willing to try anything. This is the fourth call like this I've been on this week. I know something isn't right, but as far as I can tell, they've all died of natural causes. If you can tell me different, it would make my mind a lot easier."

"This is a little out of my line," Egil explained, "but we'll be happy to give a look if it will help."

"Can we see the body?" Jack said.

"It's in the first room there. One of the other residents found him and called it in. From what we know he went out about seven o'clock. No one saw him come back in."

The room was sparsely furnished with a dresser, a side chair, and a narrow bed. The deceased was lying on the latter, composed as if in sleep except for the look of terror on the face.

Jack set his bag on the chair, opened it, and pulled out a crystal pendulum suspended from a black thread that looked as if it was human hair, which it probably was. This he held over the heart of the dead man, watching its motions as it swung back and forth.

"The body has been moved," Jack stated.

"Say what?" Dupree exclaimed.

"He didn't die here," Jack explained. "He died somewhere else and was brought here afterwards."

"How can you tell?" the man from the M.E. asked.

"This pendulum is tuned to the life force. Normally it would swing along an axis aligned with the head and feet. It's the Law of Sympathy. But as you can see, it's swinging along a diagonal. Therefore we can tell that when he died, his head was pointing in that direction. He must have died someplace else and been brought here."

"They didn't cover that in med school," the M.E. man said.

"Couldn't he have died lying that way and someone just put him to rest in the bed?" the detective asked.

"The room's too small for that."

"Any way to tell where he died, then?"

"Maybe, but let's see if we can find out what he died from first," Jack said.

He pulled four black candles from his bag and placed one on each of the four posts of the bed, lighting them in turn with a chant that Egil recognized as Sanskrit. Next he gently opened the shirt front to reveal the chest. He got a small bottle of a reddish liquid and with a small brush and drew a pentagram on the chest of the corpse, the top point set toward the head. In each point he traced a symbol of one of the planets with that of Venus set in the center over the heart.

He drew a small velvet bag out, opened it and placed a small crystal sphere in the upturned palm of his right hand. Egil knew that crystal balls are mostly for show, but this one appeared to be the real deal. Placing the sphere over each of the points of the pentagram he engaged in a one sided discussion in the Latin vulgate. Egil couldn't hear the responses, but they seemed to puzzle Jack. Finally he placed the sphere over the heart. The discussion was lengthier and more intense. Finally, Jack stood erect, and restored the ball to its bag.

"It's curious," he said. "There is no trace of a life force. Normally, some small bit will remain with a body for a number of hours after death. We know this man was alive less than four hours ago. I should have been able to detect some sign of it and by sensing in which organs it was weakest determine something about the cause of death. But in this case, the life force is completely gone. Vanished."

"Are you talking about the soul?" the detective asked.

"No. The life force is something much more primal. It is what is responsible for animating the very cells of our bodies."

"So are you saying this man died because his life force has dissipated?" the M.E. man asked. "That sounds like he's dead because he died."

"And I think that's exactly what happened," Jack said quietly.

"But how can that happen?"

"Because the life force was removed. Taken. By someone or something."

"That sounds like murder to me," the detective said.

"I agree," Jack replied.

"But how? And who?"

"As to the how, there are spells. Obviously of the Black Arts, not the White. As to who, that is a more troubling question. I suggest you find out where this man went tonight. But I would do so carefully. Whoever did this holds the power of life or death in his hands. Literally."

"So what do we do about it?" the detective queried.

"Before we can decide on that, we need to find the answer to your second question. We need to find the who," Jack responded. "Then maybe we can determine a course of action. But whoever is behind this, I don't think it is can be settled within the law."

"I don't care about that," the detective said. "This has got to be stopped by whatever means are necessary."

"Good, I hoped you would say that."

Two night later they met at Dupree's café after closing. Jack had called a council of war saying that he had new information that would shed light on the deaths.

Bubba Dupree started things off with, "I hope you've had better luck than the police have. We haven't been able to find out anything new."

"Well, I decided to do a little investigation on my own. I had a sense there might be a connection between the zombie, the attacks on Amos, and what was happening." Jack was using the word "sense" in a more specific way than just a hunch or feeling. A trained magician can perceive the presence of magic almost as a sixth sense.

"I talked to some of the men who hang out here at the café. I thought they would have an idea of what was going on. They all expressed a dread of this soup kitchen run by this man, the Rev. Isaac. They had been there and had gotten an uncomfortable feeling about the place. Nothing specific, but they just didn't like it. So I decided to check it out.

"I disguised myself as a poor old man," Jack said. It was all Egil could do to keep from smiling. No matter whatever his current motif, "poor old man" was usually a pretty good description of his friend. "I disguised myself and went down there for the free food. Amos is right, the food there isn't nearly as good as his. Of course, with their cook turned into a zombie they might not be at their best."

"I did some asking around about the zombie. He used to work at the soup kitchen regularly, kind of as head chef, prepping things before going to work at the restaurant every day. There didn't seem anything wrong with him."

"Anyway, the first time I went there it was for the lunch. Not much, just bread and soup, but the food was ok. Nothing wrong with it that I could tell. But when I came back in the evening, it was a different story.

"First thing is the crowd was different. At lunch, they had been ok. Old and poor, but they had their wits about them. The crowd at night was different. More dissipated or suffering from mental problems. It was like the smart ones avoided dinner. Only the ones that had given up hope showed up in the evening.

"Then, they didn't hand out the food right away. First we had to sit through a sermon by this Rev. Isaac. That's when I noticed it. He wasn't human. Oh, his body might have been human once, but what was in there now was pure demon, and not a nice one. He made his speech.

Talked quite a while, then we were allowed to get the dinner. A gumbo with some strong sausage.

"I could tell that there was something wrong with it. I managed to grab a sample, but that might have been a mistake. I think one of the people working saw me. But there was something in the gumbo. Extract from the puffer fish. Not much, not enough to affect you with one helping. But if you ate there every night for a few weeks, it would build up."

"So you think they're trying to make zombies?"

"No. I think that's just to make the diners more pliable. After I took the sample, they were watching me, so I had to eat at least a little of the gumbo. It definitely had an effect. The dinner broke up about ten and they ushered people out. All except one old guy. He was pretty far gone. When he tried to get up from his seat one of the helpers just pushed him back down again. He just sat and didn't move. Not a zombie, but his will had been taken from him.

"I didn't see what happened then, because a couple of big guys came up and said I had to leave. After the fugu extract I was in no position to do anything, anyway. So I left. I read in the paper this morning that they found another dead body. There was a picture. It was him."

"So you think that this Rev. Isaac killed him? What for?"

"The demon inside of him is feeding on the life force of the dead men, and with every death he grows stronger."

"Damn," Bubba said. "I ain't afraid of no man, but demons, now that's something else again. How do you go about stopping a demon?"

"That's why I called you all here. There are ways to stop a demon, but they call for planning and care. And I don't need to add that they are extremely dangerous."

"If you think you can stop this thing, count me in," the detective stated.

"Egil?" Jack asked. "Can I count on you as well? This may be more dangerous than anything we've faced before."

"I'm in."

"Good. Tomorrow is a full moon. Such times create special conditions. Not just the tides of the sea, but tides between our world and that of the demons. If we can lure this Rev. Isaac to a place of our choosing, it may be possible to cast the demon out of this world and back to where it came from."

"Won't it just come back?" Amos Dupree asked.

"Crossing over is easier said than done. Particularly for a demon. It requires massive amounts of energy. If we can weaken the demon in the process it may be decades, even centuries before it can return."

"You said a place of our choosing," Bubba Dupree said. "Where would that be?"

"I thought that would have been obvious," Jack said with just the hint of a smile. "A graveyard."

"Of course," the detective responded. "Lord, what have I gotten myself into?"

The Twelfth Street Cemetery was the oldest in the city. Originally located on the outskirts, the city had grown and enveloped it so that it was a green oasis surrounded by blocks of buildings. While it housed the graves and monuments of the oldest and most important families, it also held the original pauper's field where the poor and indigent had been buried for over a century.

During the day it was a sea of tranquility, the ordered rows of headstones guarded by ancient oaks. At night, particularly during a full moon, the atmosphere was completely different. It became a land of shadows, the tombstones and mausoleums dark menacing forms, the quiet that was so peaceful during the day turning oppressive and ominous.

Two main lanes divided the cemetery, one running more or less east-west, the other north-south and meeting in what was for all purposes the geographic center of the burying place. To the northeast lay the graves of the indigent, marked, if at all, by simple stones or plaques. The southwest quadrant contained the monuments and crypts of the wealthy and notable. It was at these crossroads that Jack and Egil had positioned themselves and made their preparations.

At the center of the crossroads Jack had drawn a large pentacle inscribed in a circle. Each point of the pentagram held a symbol of power. In the center of each of the four converging lanes was drawn another circle with appropriate symbols marking the four cardinal points. Various objects and instruments awaited them inside the center of the pentacle.

"Are your men in position and have they been given their instructions?" Jack asked the detective.

"There's a squad car with two men at each of the four gates. They've been told to let Rev. Isaac enter the grounds and then shut the gates behind him. They've all got radios to stay in communications. All of the foot gates have been locked and marked as well."

"Good. On no condition are they to enter the cemetery once the demon enters."

"They've been told. I still don't understand how you are so sure that Rev. Isaac will be coming," the detective said.

"He'll be here because I invited him," Jack answered simply.

"You invited him?"

"Let's say I made him an offer he couldn't refuse," Jack said. "These things have rules. If we are to succeed we must play by those rules. The demon has been challenged. Therefore it must come. Trust me."

"I do. Lord help me, I do."

"It's almost midnight, time for us to take our places."

"Where do you want me?" Bubba Dupree asked.

"I've prepared a place of safety in the doorway of that mausoleum over there," Jack said pointing to a marble edifice that stood just off to the side. "You'll be able to observe and communicate with your men from there. You'll be as safe as I can make it. But, whatever you do, don't come out of the doorway until I tell you it's ok. And if things go wrong, stay there until dawn. Do you understand?"

"No, but I'll do it."

"Good. Now Egil, it's time for us to close the pentacle."

The detective walked off to his sanctuary. Jack and Egil entered the pentagram, closing first the circle, then the pentacle itself, with a flourish, sealing the characters with the blood of a goat.

The night had been cloudy, but as the hour of midnight approached, the dark masses parted to reveal the pale orb of the full moon. No breath of breeze disturbed the graveyard. The two men waited within the fragile safety of the pentacle.

From the mausoleum they could hear the crackle of the detectives radio. "He's coming," Dupree called out.

Along the south lane they could see the dark form of a black limousine driving without its lights. It stopped just short of the crossroads. A tall, thin form emerged from the back seat and walked towards the waiting wizards.

The Rev. Isaac was a skeletal figure nearly seven feet tall dressed in a long tailcoat of a style that had gone out of fashion decades earlier. A top hat stood on his head exaggerating his height. His skin was almost black, broken only by the whites of his eyes and the leer of his teeth.

"Who dares to challenge the power of Baron Samedi in the very heart of his realm?" he said in a deep booming voice as he stopped just short of the symbol marking the south entrance to the crossroads.

Egil looked uncertainly at Jack, but the older man seemed calm as he faced the demon.

"One who belongs in this world," Jack answered.

"This world," the demon asked waving his hand at the gravestones surrounding them. "If that is your wish, it can be arranged."

"The world of the mortal and the living," Jack replied.

"The world of the weak and frail. Go now, old man, before I suck the life from you."

Egil knew that Jack had been waiting for the very moment of local midnight, that instant when the moon was exactly overhead. That moment had come.

"NO!"

Though Jack had spoken the word, the sound did not seem to come from his mouth. Instead it seemed to emanate from every stone and tree in the graveyard.

"In the name of the living and the light I repudiate you."

Jack drew a silver short sword, an arthame, from his belt and using it he drew glowing characters in the air between him and the demon.

For a moment the demon seemed taken aback, then the white smile flashed in his ebon face.

"Do you thing that the powers of the Sect Roug, the Cochon gris, the Verbrindingue, fear an old man with a silver toothpick. Behold real power old man and weep."

The demon waved his hands sending the clouds scudding across the face of the moon. The air, which had been still, suddenly began to swirl around the crossroads picking up leaves and dust to form a small tornado with the heart of the pentagram as its vortex.

"There are older powers than those," Jack said. He uttered one more word, the sound of which Egil could not wrap his ears around. He knew it was an old word in a language long forgotten. As suddenly as it had appeared, the whirlwind ceased, the leaves falling to the ground. The clouds withdrew from the face of the moon and it seemed as if a silver beam came down to bathe the two figures in the center of the crossroads.

"By the sun and the moon, the earth and the air. By water and fire. I summoned you to this crossroads and I can dismiss you."

Ethereal fires seemed to rise from each of the symbols at the cardinal points marking the crossroads. This was no magic that Egil had ever seen before. It certainly was not what he had been taught at Cal Thaum. There was something primordial about it. Not for the first time he wondered just how old his friend really was.

"You want ju-ju? You want gris-gris? I'll show you power," Jack declaimed. From out of nowhere bolts of lightning struck each of the symbols putting out the fire.

The smile was gone from the Rev. Isaac's face. This was not what the demon had expected.

"You are more resourceful than I had thought, old man. I will grant you that. But know, despite this mortal form that I have put on, that I am a demon, lord of the tenth ring, a power of powers. Do you think you can match that, oh wizard?"

Jack smiled.

"In this world, you survive on borrowed power. You hang on by stealing the life force of the old and the weak. I call on you to surrender what you have stolen and return from whence you came. By stone and rock, by stream and lake, by tree and bush, by bird and animal, by all the myriad of insects that crawl in the ground. Begone!"

There was a flash. It seemed as if dozens of arrows of light were streaming out of the body of Rev. Isaac, streaming out of him and towards the pauper's field. The tall form slumped to the ground. Suddenly it was still again. In the distance came the call of an owl.

"You can relax, lad. It's over. For now," Jack said.

Casually he broke the pentacle with his foot, scrubbing out the characters that had sealed them within. They walked over to where Rev. Isaac lay on the pavement.

"You can come out now, detective."

Bubba Dupree joined them as they stood over the body.

"Is he dead?" the detective asked.

"The body is still alive. As to the other, only time will tell. The demon wore the shell for a long time. There may be nothing left to resume occupation of the body."

"But the demon? That's gone? There won't be any more old men dying?"

"The demon will not return in your lifetime. Old men will still die, but only from natural causes."

That Friday night they met again over gumbo, jambalaya, and cold beers at the New Orleans Café. Everyone was in an upbeat mood. The old men playing cards at the table in the corner had waved a greeting when they came in. It seemed as if a shadow had been lifted over the whole neighborhood.

After Amos Dupree had brought yet another dish to the table he stood and announced, "I would like to make a toast to our new friends Jack and Egil. There will always be a place for them at the table wherever I cook."

Jack nodded his acceptance and raised his glass in turn. "If the food is as good as it is tonight, you can count on my being back."

"I take it there have been no mysterious deaths?" Egil asked between mouthfuls.

"Nothing out of the ordinary, I'm happy to say," Bubba Dupree replied. "And you'll be happy to know that William Johnston is out of the hospital and back working at Francois's. Though from what I hear, that place may not be in business much longer."

"And Rev. Isaac? How is he doing?"

"The doctors aren't hopeful. The body is functioning, but his mind seems to be gone. They are moving him to the state hospital."

"I doubt it will ever return," Jack said soberly. "For all intents and purposes he has become what he tried to make of Johnston, a zombie."

"Enough of this down talk," Amos said. "This is supposed to be a celebration. I've got one more dish for you and then desert. Does anyone need another beer?"

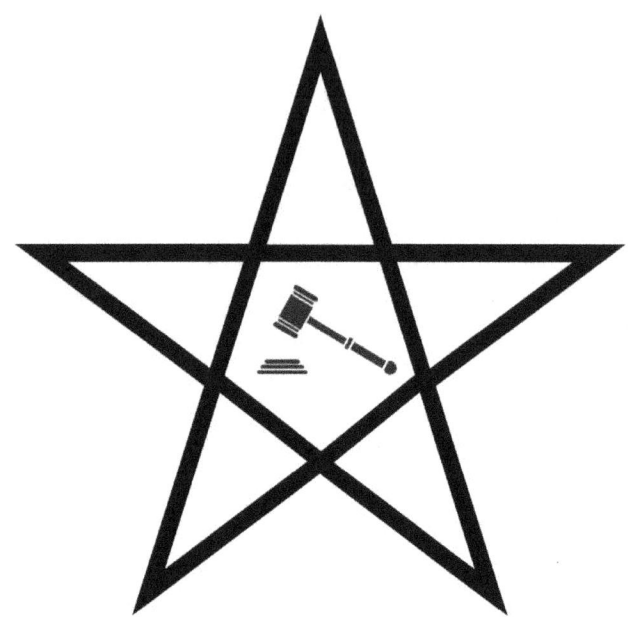

MAGIC ON TRIAL

MAGIC ON TRIAL

☆　☆　☆　☆　☆

"Place your hand on the orb. Do you swear to tell the truth, the whole truth, and nothing but the truth?"

"I do." The orb took on a solid green glow. The court clerk seemed satisfied, and restored the orb to its stand on his desk.

"Please state your full name and occupation," he said, facing the witness.

"Egil Grim Njalsson. I am an attorney at law."

"The prosecution may proceed," the judge said from his place on the bench.

"Thank you, your honor." Addressing the witness, Adam Cline, the prosecutor, continued, "Mr. Njalsson. You have stated that you are an attorney. Can you please tell us what areas, if any, of the law you specialize in?"

"I have experience in all areas of the law," the witness responded, "but much of my practice deals with the laws of intellectual property, in particular those matters relating to the magical arts."

"In other words your work deals with such matters as patents on spells and magical processes?"

"That is correct."

"And besides your training in the law, do you have any special qualifications for this admittedly esoteric specialty?"

"I hold a Bachelor of Science degree in metaphysics from the California Institute of Thaumaturgy."

"For those members of the jury unfamiliar with this institution, CalThaum, as it is known, is perhaps the preeminent institution of higher learning specializing in the science and technology of magic in the country. Would you say that is a fair assessment, Mr. Njalsson?"

"It certainly is one of the top in those fields."

"Which is more than can be said of their football team, the 'Wizards'." Cline remarked jokingly to the audience. For those who pay attention to such matters, the CalThaum Wizards were perhaps the worst collegiate team in the sport. They were also, perhaps , the only team whose average IQ was greater than their average weight. The team's current losing streak was at thirty four and counting.

"Then, Mr. Njalsson, as a graduate of CalThaum, you are a fully qualified wizard?"

"Yes," Egil answered. He was finding the experience of being a witness interesting. He had, of course testified as a technical expert on a number of occasions, but this was his first time as a witness in a criminal case.

"And you are also licensed to practice magic?"

"I hold a first class commercial magic license in this state."

"Thank you, Mr. Njalsson. I would like the jury, as we discuss subsequent matters, to bear in mind that the witness is an expert not only in the law but in the magical arts."

"Now, Mr. Njalsson, are you familiar with the work of Dr. Ernest Haverly?"

"Yes."

"And in fact you were employed by that gentleman, were you not?"

"That is correct."

"I'd like you to tell us exactly what was the nature of your business with Dr. Haverly."

"Dr. Haverly had developed a new magical process. He consulted me in regards to patenting this process."

"Which, as we have established, is an area in which you are experienced, and in fact have something of a reputation. Is that correct?"

"Yes." Egil was having difficulty seeing exactly where Cline's questions were going, but then his criminal law experience was limited, especially from a prosecutor's standpoint.

"Dr. Haverly himself has quite a reputation in academic circles, doesn't he, Mr. Njalsson?"

"Yes, I believe he does."

"And you, with your scientific background, would be able to appreciate this more than the average layman. Would you not?"

"Probably."

"Perhaps you could explain for the members of the jury exactly what Dr. Haverly is so well known for?"

"I won't pretend I really understand the details," Egil said. "His work was far beyond anything I was exposed to as an undergraduate. But Dr. Haverly is probably the world's foremost expert in the subject of transmutation."

"By transmutation, you mean the changing of one element into another, for example, lead into gold."

"Yes."

"But I thought that was impossible."

"Oh no, it's quite possible. As far back as 1847, Helmholz was able to achieve the transmutation of lead to gold. However, Helmholz's process is so expensive in terms of materials and energy that it has never been considered economically feasible. Interestingly, theoretically the transmutation of gold into lead is quite simple, but for obvious reasons has never been pursued."

"Yes, thank you, Mr. Njalsson," Cline interrupted. "So Dr. Haverly had invented a process for transmuting lead into gold?"

"No. As I said, that is not an economically viable process, and probably never will be for reasons having to do with the relative atomic weights of the two elements. Dr. Haverly was working on a much more practical process, that of transmuting silicon into aluminum."

"But aluminum is quite abundant," Cline objected.

"Yes, but the process to refine it from bauxite ore is quite expensive in terms of the energy consumed. Whereas, Dr. Haverly's process takes a fairly pure substance that is readily available, which is sand, and converts it into refined aluminum while using perhaps a tenth of the energy that the traditional process using bauxite ore does."

"So this process has economic potential?"

"Certainly. Consider just the amount of aluminum required by the beverage industry each year. The process is potentially worth millions."

"And so it is a secret that Dr. Haverly has a great interest in protecting?"

"Yes. Of course. That's why he consulted me about the patent application for the process and spells involved. He wanted to make sure that all aspects of the process were protected and that there was no way around the patents."

"Now, Mr. Njalsson, you have stated that this process of Dr. Haverly's was potentially worth millions. Were you aware of any negotiations the doctor had engaged in to market this process?"

"He informed me that he wanted to perfect the process and secure the patent rights before he entered into any negotiations. However, he also had told me that news of his work had leaked out and he had been approached by at least one party who had attempted to purchase the rights."

"And what was his response to this offer?"

"He had refused. From what he said, the offer was substantially less than what he believed it was worth."

"Did he mention who had made this offer?" the prosecutor asked.

"He said his name was Alan Rigsby who was acting as an agent for a company called Consolidated Investments."

"After Dr. Haverly refused this offer, did this Alan Rigsby make a counter offer?"

"I believe there were several additional offers. Rigsby seemed to be very determined."

"And Dr. Haverly refused each of these offers?"

"Yes. He had investigated Consolidated Investments and decided that they did not have the best reputation."

"Exactly what did you think he meant by that, Mr. Njalsson."

"I believe certain allegations had been made in the past about their business practices—allegations of threats and intimidation used to secure agreements. However, to my knowledge, nothing has ever been proved."

"Did Dr. Haverly indicate that this Rigsby had tried to intimidate him?"

"Not in so many words, but he had implied that 'pressure' was being applied," Egil answered.

"Did Dr. Haverly seemed concerned by this?"

"No. When I suggested he approach the authorities he assured me he could handle things on his own."

"Thank you, Mr. Njalsson. Now I'd like to turn to the events of June 13 of this year. I believe that you had an appointment with Dr. Haverly?"

"Yes, that is correct."

"And what was the nature of this appointment? Did he wish to discuss the patent application?"

"No. Not directly. He had some concerns about the security of his papers. There had been several attempts to steal the secret of his process."

"So he wished to consult you not as his lawyer, but as a wizard. Is that correct?"

"Yes."

"Do you frequently act as a consulting wizard on security matters?"

"From time to time, yes."

"Are you an expert in the field?"

"I am familiar with most of the commercial security spells and devices. I also have developed a few tricks of my own over the years. As I handle a great deal of proprietary information, my clients are concerned with its security."

"So you were to meet with Dr. Haverly at his laboratory to review his security precautions?"

"That is a reasonable way to put it."

"Were you to meet him alone?"

"No. I was accompanied by a colleague."

"One Jakob Schmidts, I believe. Is he a practicing wizard, as well?"

"He does have a Third Class Commercial license."

"That doesn't sound particularly impressive, Mr. Njalsson."

"Mr. Schmidts is something of an old school magician," Egil responded with a smile. "While he may be lacking in some of the academic areas of the art, he has a wide range of knowledge in its more traditional aspects. I find that knowledge quite useful at times, and have consulted him on a number of occasions."

"I see," Cline responded a bit uncertainly. He continued, "Getting back to the night of June 13, can you tell us what transpired."

"I picked up Mr. Schmidts at his place of business. I think it was around seven o'clock. We drove to Dr. Haverly's residence. His laboratory is in a separate building at the rear of the grounds. We parked the car and then walked to the laboratory, where Dr. Haverly said he was going to meet us. I rang the bell at the entrance, but there was no response. This caused me some concern as Dr. Haverly is normally a very precise and prompt individual."

"What happened next, Mr. Njalsson? Did you leave?"

"No. As I say, I was concerned. I tried the door and found that it was unlocked. This only increased my unease as Dr. Haverly is a very careful person. People who work with dangerous magics usually are. At least if they are at it for very long."

"So you found the door unlocked which was unusual. Did you consider calling the police?"

"Not at that point. In the first instance, it would take them some time to respond. In the second, if nothing was wrong, it might draw a certain amount of attention which Dr. Haverly was trying to avoid until the patent issues were settled."

"So what did you do?"

"Jake and I undertook a magical investigation of the door."

"I see. Your client has missed a meeting, and in your mind may have met with foul play and you stop to examine the door. What were you expecting to find, Mr. Njalsson?"

"Booby-traps. Either magical or non-magical."

"And did you find any?"

"No. Though both of us sensed that there was a great deal of magical energy present. Of course, given the nature of Dr. Haverly's work, that wasn't entirely unexpected."

"How long did this examination take?"

"A minute, perhaps two."

"What did you do then?"

"I pushed opened the door and called out to Dr. Haverly."

"You didn't enter?"

"Not at first."

"Did you get a response to your call?"

"Not at first. I tried a second time and heard a faint cry from the back of the building. It sounded like Dr. Haverly's voice saying 'Is that you, Njalsson?' But it was very weak."

"Don't keep us in suspense, Mr. Njalsson. What did you do next?"

"We entered the building. The laboratory consists of several rooms. The front is a sort of office or study. Next comes a laboratory, and behind that is a big open room for large scale experiments that will not fit on a table. There was no one is either the study or the lab. We walked through the lab. It has a number of benches and tables. We checked behind those to make sure Dr. Haverly wasn't concealed behind them."

"You thought he might be injured?"

"The possibility crossed my mind. His voice had sounded weak."

"What next?"

"When we were sure he was not in the laboratory, we went on into the room in the back. This is separated from the lab by a large, heavy door. It was almost closed. I pushed it open. That was when I saw Dr. Haverly. He was lying on the ground, just barely conscious."

"Did you see any marks upon him? Was there any sign that there had been a struggle?"

"No. He was unmarked. As to whether a struggle had taken place—it was hard to tell. The room is unfurnished, just a large space. Nothing to be over turned or upset."

"Seeing Dr. Haverly lying on the ground did you go to him?"

"Not at first. He was lying at the center of a pentagram that had been drawn on the floor of the room. It was obviously there as some form of protection. We thought that it might be dangerous to both ourselves and Dr. Haverly if we disturbed it without taking precautions."

"I see. Are such—pentagrams—usual?"

"Yes. Quite often they are needed to protect the magician when working on a spell."

"I understand that these pentagrams can be quite elaborate and that it may take some time to construct."

"Yes, that is true. Depending, of course, on exactly what forces are involved."

"But you, yourself, have constructed such pentagrams?"

"Yes. A number of times."

"In your estimate, how long would it have taken Dr. Haverly to draw this particular pentagram?"

"Perhaps several minutes."

"So it was not a spur of the moment sort of thing."

"No. It was quite deliberate. You must keep in mind, though, that Dr. Haverly is a very experienced and knowledgeable wizard."

"Yes, I will. And I will remind the jury to keep that in mind as well. Now what happened next?"

"As Mr. Schmidts and I were examining the pentagram trying to decide what our best approach was, Dr. Haverly seemed to revive just a bit. Seeing our predicament, he rose up just enough to reach the signing sigil and erase it."

"I'm not sure I understand. Could you explain?

"When constructing a pentagram, the final step is usually to draw an elaborate figure to seal the pentagram. It's sort of a signature, but also a key. If the sigil is broken or erased, the power of the pentagram is disarmed. This is what happened when Dr. Haverly wiped out the sigil. We were then able to enter the pentagram and reach him."

"And in what condition did you find him?"

"He was very weak. Exhausted, but, otherwise in good shape."

"And what do you attribute this exhaustion to?"

"I'm not sure."

"Isn't it true that the wielding of great magical power can exhaust a magician?"

"Yes, that is true."

"Could Dr. Haverly's condition be explained by his having just executed a particularly powerful spell?"

"Yes. That's possible."

"Did you see anything else in the room besides the pentagram and Dr. Haverly?"

"Yes. There was what I at first took to be a statue of some sort."

"Can you describe this statue?"

"It was the life size figure of a man. About five foot nine, I'd say. It appeared to be made out of glass or quartz or some such transparent material."

"In fact, Mr. Njalsson, it wasn't a statue, was it?"

"No, it wasn't," Egil answered with a visible shudder.

"What, in fact, was it?"

"Later examination proved it to be the body of a man, except that all of the carbon atoms in his body had been converted to silicon."

"The statue was in reality, Alan Rigsby, who had been transmuted from a living, breathing man into a pillar of quartz. Is that not the case, Mr. Njalsson?"

"Objection!," Walter Greenwood, council for the defense interjected. "The prosecution is purposefully using inflammatory language to make unproved assertions."

"Sustained," the judge said. "The witness is not required to answer the question. Gentlemen. Seeing as it is nearly eleven thirty I suggest we take a break for lunch. Are there any objections? No? Then the court is adjourned until one P.M. this afternoon."

☆   ☆   ☆   ☆   ☆

"All rise. The Third District Court, the Honorable Edward Wilson presiding is now in session."

The judge entered and took his seat behind the bench. "Mr. Cline, you may proceed."

"Your Honor, I would like to temporarily excuse Mr. Njalsson and call another witness. I wish to do so in order to present the facts of the events of the night of June 13 to the jury more clearly."

"Mr. Greenwood," the judge said turning to the defense council, "Do you have any objections?"

"No, your Honor, as long as it is understood that I may recall the witness at a later date for further questioning."

"Granted. Mr. Cline, you may proceed."

"The prosecution would like to call Jakob Schmidts to the stand."

The bailiff escorted the next witness to the stand. He was a thin man of somewhat indeterminate age, though clearly not young, average height and curiously mutable features. He was wearing a suit that at one time had been of high quality but now appeared somewhat shabby and dated.

"Place your hand on the orb. Do you swear to tell the truth, the whole truth, and nothing but the truth?"

What happened next struck those familiar with the magic surrounding the orb as decidedly strange. It certainly caused the clerk a degree of consternation, for the orb, rather than glowing with its normal green took on a distinct bluish tint, the likes of which the clerk had never seen before in his twenty years in court. He looked uncertainly up at the judge who seemed to have chosen not to notice the oddity.

"Please state your full name and occupation," the clerk continued after deciding no other course was open to him.

"Jakob Elihu Schmidts," the witness stated in a remarkably clear and powerful voice. "Dealer in second hand merchandise."

"Isn't it true, Mr. Schmidts," the prosecutor asked, "that in addition to your business as an antiques dealer you also practice the magical arts on the side?"

"If you mean, do I tell the occasional fortune or read tea leaves and such, then the answer is yes. And I have a Third Class Magician's license that allows me to do so." The witness seemed in no way cowed by the prosecutor.

"And you are acquainted with the previous witness, Egil Njalsson?"

"If you mean is the lad a friend of mine, yes. He's kind enough to bring an old man the occasional bottle and while away the evening with conversation." For a moment, Schmidts speech had taken on a hint of an Irish brogue.

"And these conversations are often about magical topics?"

"Sometimes. Egil is a clever enough lad to understand that not everything about The Art is taught in that fancy school he went to. He sometimes has questions about some of the more obscure facets of lore that only an old hedge wizard might know."

"That would explain why a graduate of CalThaum and a First Class Magician would consult a, as you put it, hedge wizard?"

"As I said, the lad is clever." The prosecutor did not seem pleased. The questioning was not going quite as he had intended.

"Can you please tell the jury how it is that you came to accompany Mr. Njalsson to the residence of Dr. Haverly on the night of June 13?" he asked, trying to steer the testimony back on course.

"It seems that this Dr. Haverly was concerned about the security of his premises. He was working on some new process that he thought might be quite valuable and was worried that someone was out to steal it. He had asked Egil to check his security spells and wards and such. Egil asked me along to give him a hand."

"Is he often in the habit of consulting you on such matters? Mr. Njalsson, I mean."

"On occasion. You see, I know a few tricks that aren't common knowledge. Sometimes the old ways are the best ways, particularly if the young fellers aren't familiar with them."

"I see. Are you aware of the nature of the work that Dr. Haverly was engaged in?"

"From what Egil told me, he was working on a spell that would transmute silicon into aluminum. Now personally, I prefer my liquid refreshment in bottles as was intended, but there are some that like the convenience of aluminum cans."

"And are you aware of Dr. Haverly's reputation in his field?"

"I've read a few of his papers, yes. Very clever work, too. You can tell he understands his subject."

"You say you read his papers. What exactly do you mean by that? Were you privy to his latest research?"

"No. I meant his scholarly works. You know like publications in *The Metaphysical Review* and *Metaphysical Letters*. There was an interesting discussion in the latter about Helmholz's original transmutation spell."

The prosecutor for a moment seemed nonplused with the old man's response.

"You say that you read some of the accused's publications. I was given to believe by Mr. Njalsson's testimony that they were quite, shall we say, esoteric in nature."

"Oh, Egil's a smart lad, alright, but these days he's more concerned with his lawyering than with keeping up with the latest in The Art. Me, I'm an old man with a lot of time on his hands. I can afford to spend my time reading journals and the like. Just because I'm an old man, doesn't mean I don't know a thing or two about mathematics and metaphysics."

"I apologize, Mr. Schmidts, for underestimating you. To get back to the night of June 13, you accompanied Mr. Njalsson in order to check Dr. Haverly's security arrangements?

"That is correct."

"In your own words, can you describe what you found when you arrived?"

"Well, we drove out in Egil's car. Parked it out front, and then walked around to the lab which is a separate building in the back of the property. Egil rang the bell, but there was no answer. He tried it several times and then tried the door. It was unlocked. We both thought that a bit strange. People that are concerned about their security don't usually leave their doors unlocked."

"What did you do next?"

"Well, like I said, the door was unlocked. We opened it and went in. Egil called out Dr. Haverly's name a couple of times. Then we heard a faint voice from the back of the lab. I couldn't make out what it was saying, but Egil seemed to think it was Dr. Haverly's. I wouldn't know, as I'd never met the man before. But it sounded like he was sick or injured."

"What happened then?"

"We started going through the building towards the back. It's kind of arranged as three rooms. There's a sort of study in the front by the entrance, then a laboratory room, and then in the rear a big open space, maybe twenty by forty feet. There was no one in the study, so we went into the laboratory. There wasn't anyone there, so then we went into the back room."

"And what did you find there?" the prosecutor asked.

"We saw Dr. Haverly lying on the ground at the center of a pentagram, and a prettier piece of work I've never seen before. The man knows a thing or two about protection spells. The place was heavy with magic. I could smell it."

"When you say you could smell it, do you mean it had a distinctive odor?"

"Not exactly. And it's not really smelling in the normal sense of the word. It's just that if you've worked a lot of magic over the years you can sort of sense when it's been used. Some are better at it than others, like witch smellers are particularly keen at it."

"So you saw Dr. Haverly in the middle of a pentagram and you say the 'smell' of magic was heavy in the air. What was Dr. Haverly's condition?"

"He looked like he was only half conscious. Like I said he was lying in the middle of the pentagram."

"To what did you attribute his condition?"

"I didn't know for sure, but sometimes when a magician works particularly big spell it drains a lot of energy out of him."

"Objection," the defense council declared. "This is pure conjecture on the part of the witness."

"Sustained," the judge decreed. "The jury will disregard the last statement by the witness."

"What else did you see in the room?"

"There wasn't any furniture or anything. Off against the wall was a bag that contained some apparatus and supplies that Dr. Haverly had used to draw the pentagram and work whatever spell he had done."

"Objection. It is only the witnesses opinion that Dr. Haverly worked a spell, or that any spell had been worked at all."

"Your honor, we have already established that Mr. Schmidts has some experience with magic and is a licensed practitioner. One can reasonably infer that he is competent to recognize whether a spell has occurred or not."

"Over ruled, Mr. Greenwood. The defense may raise the question of the witness's competence on the subject during cross-examination. You may continue, Mr. Cline."

"Thank you, your Honor," Cline said bowing to the judge. "Now, Mr. Schmidts, was there anything else in this back room?"

"There was life size statue thing made out of glass or quartz, only when I got a close look at it, I could see it wasn't any statue. It was a man."

"Did you recognize the 'statue'?"

"I did not."

"I ask you to look at this photo and compare it to your memories of this statue," the prosecutor said displaying an eight by ten photograph to the witness.

"That has the likeness of the statue."

"Let the record state that the photograph is of Alan Rigsby."

"Now, what happened next?"

"Well, neither Egil or I felt we should break the pentagram where Dr. Haverly lay. As I said, it looked to be a very powerful piece of work and we weren't sure what might happen if we forced our way into it. Fortunately, Dr. Haverly came to his senses enough to erase the sigil signing the pentagram, thus dissolving its power. With it safe, Egil and I went to his side. He was weak, but otherwise appeared to be unharmed."

"Did Dr. Haverly say anything to either of you at this time?"

"He said, 'I did it, didn't I?'"

"To what did you think he was referring?"

"He was looking at the statue."

"I have no further questions for the witness at this time, your Honor."

"Mr. Greenwood. Do you wish to cross examine the witness."

"I do." Walter Greenwood rose from his position behind the defense table. Unlike the prosecutor who had worn a serious expression during the testimony, the attorney for the defense had an affable air about him, looking like nothing so much as a kindly uncle, an image he studiously tried to maintain at all times in court.

"Now, Mr. Schmidts, we have established that you have some considerable talent at sensing the presence of magic due to your considerable experience in the field. Is that correct?"

"I won't deny it."

"And you say that when you entered the back room of Dr. Haverly's laboratory you could sense the presence of strong magics. Were you able to distinguish just how many spells had occurred and their origins?"

"Objection," Cline exclaimed. "This calls for conjecture on the part of the witness."

"I don't think you can have it two ways, Mr. Cline," responded the judge. "You have already relied on Mr. Schmidts competence in earlier testimony. You can't deny the defense the same opportunity. Objection overruled. Continue Mr. Greenwood."

"Please answer my last question, Mr. Schmidts."

"There were certainly multiple spells that had taken place. I couldn't tell for certain how many, but there were at least three major ones. One I attributed to the pentagram in which we found Dr. Haverly."

"To interrupt you for a moment, a pentagram, such as the one you found Dr. Haverly at the center of, is a defensive mechanism, is it not?"

"Yes. It was plainly a defense against a magical or demonic attack."

"And being protective, it did not have any offensive capabilities, did it."

"Not unless one was trying to breach it by force. Then the results could be rather nasty."

"Go on. You said that you sensed at least three spells. Could you tell what the others were."

"There was a second spell. It was not generated by Dr. Haverly. Every wizard has a particular signature. I knew his from the pentagram. The second spell was cast by someone or something else and I believe it was directed against the pentagram protecting Dr. Haverly."

"Objection. Conjecture on the part of the witness."

"Overruled."

"So Dr. Haverly had sought to protect himself within his pentagram and someone was trying to breech this spell?"

"Yes."

"And what of the third spell?"

"That emanated from Dr. Haverly."

"You know this from the 'signature'?"

"That is correct."

"And what was the nature of this spell?"

"It was focused on the statue."

"The one that resembled Alan Rigsby."

"That's right."

"And could you discern the purpose of this spell?"

"I could not. I had never come across anything like it. The closest thing I'd ever experienced was a long time ago when I saw a man try to change lead into gold."

"So, Mr. Schmidts, the events of June 13 are consistent with the accused, Dr. Haverly, fearing some malign force, trying to protect himself, first with a passive defense in the form of a protective pentagram, and then, when it appeared that that might fail him, by launching a transmutation spell of some power against his attacker. Is that correct?"

"Objection. You Honor, this question calls on the witness to make conjectures about the accused motives as well as the sequence of his actions."

"I'm afraid I will have to sustain the prosecution's objection, Mr. Greenwood. Do you have any further questions?"

"Mr. Schmidts," Greenwood said, conspicuously consulting his notes, "in your earlier testimony you referred to the possibility of a demonic power being involved in the spell against the pentagram, and of the attack being initiated by someone or something. What exactly did you mean by that?"

"I thought I sensed a dark force behind the spell."

"By dark force do you mean 'Black Magic'?"

"I do."

"And do you have experience with black magic? I thought that the study and practice of black magic was illegal."

"It is, and rightly so. But that isn't to say that there aren't those willing to use it. I won't practice the Black Arts myself, but that doesn't mean that I haven't studied ways to counter it."

"And you think that in your words 'someone or something' was trying to breech the protection of the pentagram that Dr. Haverly had drawn on the floor of his laboratory?"

"Objection."

"Sustained," the judge said wearily.

"No further questions, your Honor."

☆   ☆   ☆   ☆   ☆

"Will the witness please state their full name and occupation?"

"Edgar James Somersby. I am Vice President of New Projects for Consolidated Investments."

"Could you briefly describe the nature of what you do for Consolidated Investments, Mr. Somersby?" the prosecutor asked.

"Put simply, Consolidated Investments provides start up money for emerging technologies in return for a portion of any eventual profits. My job is to discover new technologies and secure the intellectual property rights."

"And were you aware of Dr. Haverly's work? Was it one of the emerging technologies you were interested in?"

'I was, of course, aware of Dr. Haverly's reputation. He is well known in academic circles. We had approached him on several occasions to discuss the possibilities of his recent research."

"Did you contact him personally?"

"No. I can't possibly talk to each potential inventor. In this case Consolidated employed an independent agent to handle the preliminary discussions. I would of course have gotten involved if things had gotten serious."

"And what was the name of this agent?"

"Alan Rigsby. We had engaged him on a number of occasions."

"And how were the discussions going?"

"Dr. Haverly at first expressed reluctance, but Rigsby had indicated in our last conversation that he thought he would be able to persuade him to reach an agreement over the rights to his spell."

"And when was this conversation?"

"The twelfth of June. He indicated that he had arranged for a meeting with Haverly the next evening at Haverly's laboratory."

"And so Rigsby had a business meeting scheduled on June 13 at the laboratory."

"That is correct."

"No further questions, your Honor."

Walter Greenwood stood up, a somewhat portly figure, and looked for a moment at the witness.

"Mr. Somersby. You say that Consolidated had engaged Mr. Rigsby on several previous occasions. Is that correct?"

"Yes. I'm not sure exactly how many times."

"Were you aware of the man's criminal record?"

"It is my understanding that he had no criminal record. I believe he had been arrested several times but that in all cases the charges had been dropped."

"In fact, the charges had been dropped when witnesses had refused to testify, or in at least one case, had disappeared. Is that not the case?"

"I wouldn't know. You'd have to ask the prosecuting attorneys why the cases were dropped."

"Were you aware of the methods that Mr. Rigsby employed to persuade Dr. Haverly or others to transfer the rights to their intellectual property to Consolidated Investments?"

"Mr. Rigsby assured us that everything he did was legal. We were prepared to pay Dr. Haverly handsomely for the rights to his spell."

"On what basis was Mr. Rigsby to be rewarded if he was successful?"

"He would receive a fee based on the amount that was negotiated for securing the rights."

"So he would receive more if Consolidated paid less?"

"Yes. Obviously we are interested in maximizing our profits."

"No further questions."

☆   ☆   ☆   ☆   ☆

"The prosecution calls Dr. Harlow Manly."

The doctor appeared, a small, somewhat fussy individual. After the swearing in and the doctor identifying himself as the medical examiner for the city the prosecution began its examination.

"You examined the curious remains taken from the laboratory of Dr. Haverly, did you not?"

"Yes, I did."

"And what did you discover?"

"At first, I was puzzled as to why they had been brought to my attention. The object that was brought to my attention appeared to be a statue made of a glassy substance. However, on closer examination, the statue appeared to have much more detail than one would expect in such an object. For example, there were the presence of pores in the skin, small scars, dirt underneath the fingernails. It did not seem likely that any sculptor would go to such lengths. It occurred to me, at least as a working hypothesis, that the statue was in fact a body."

"What did you do then."

"I proceeded to do a postmortem examination. This was made difficult by the nature of the material, but with the aid of rock cutting saws I was able to make several transections through the torso and skull. These revealed the presence of all the expected internal organs. By chemical analysis, I was able to determine that the chemical makeup of the object was consistent with that of a human body in which all of the atoms of carbon had been exchanged for atoms of silicon."

"What would be the result of such a substitution on a living person."

"Instant death. All organic processes would cease to function immediately."

"And to what do you attribute this exchange of carbon for silicon?"

"I have no explanation. Such an occurrence is outside my experience, nor have I found a similar case in the literature. The only thing remotely like it is the biblical story of Lot's wife, but of course that involved sodium and not silicon."

"And were you able to discover the identity of the body, Dr. Manly?

"DNA, of course, was useless. However, the body had a full set of fingerprints and I was able to determine the identity through them. The body was that of one Alan Rigsby."

"Thank you, doctor. I have no further questions."

"Mr. Greenwood?"

"Just two points I'd like to clarify, your Honor. Dr. Manly, you say you identified the body by use of its fingerprints. How did you obtain a match?"

"I ran them through the police database. That's standard procedure."

"And you found Mr. Rigsby's fingerprints in the police files?"

"Yes."

"Do you happen to know what crime Mr. Rigsby had been accused of to cause his fingerprints to appear in the police files?"

"I believe there were a number of arrests for various offenses. Extortion, assault, grand-theft, if I remember correctly. You can check the files yourself if you want to be sure."

"Oh, I think the jury will be willing to accept your recollection. Now, Dr. Manly, were there any anatomical anomalies about the corpse, other than the fact that it was composed largely of silicon, of course?"

"There was one odd thing. It didn't come out in the initial autopsy as there was no particular reason to check for it, and given the difficult nature of working on the corpse there were limits to the examination that I made. But later, following a suggestion made by Mr. Njalsson, I made a section through the left foot."

"And what was it that you discovered during this subsequent examination?"

"I discovered that there was a curious deformation of the left foot, a deformation that was cleverly concealed by a specially formed shoe on that foot."

"And what was the nature of this deformation, Dr. Manly?"

"Instead of the normal ankle and foot structure, the bones of the left foot were shortened and bifurcated so that the deceased was essentially standing on the tips of two toes of his left foot."

"That sounds very unusual, Dr. Manly. Could you perhaps describe this anomaly in terms that would make it easier for the jury to envision?"

"Well, and this is of course just an approximation, but the closest structure that I can think of would be the hoof of an animal such as a goat."

"In other words, a cloven hoof?"

"Yes. That would be one way of thinking of it."

"No further questions, your Honor."

☆ ☆ ☆ ☆ ☆

"Mr. Greenwood, are you prepared to present the case for the defense?"

"I am, your honor," the defense council announced in a ponderous but dignified manner.

"At this time the defense would like to call Egil Njalsson to the stand," Walter Greenwood said in his best oratorical voice. Cline, the prosecutor looked uncomfortable, but he realized that his earlier agreement to interrupt Njalsson's testimony had opened him up to this maneuver with the prosecution's star witness. Judge Wilson merely looked amused.

As Njalsson took the stand the judge remarked, "I will remind the witness that he is still under oath."

"I understand your Honor."

"Now, Mr. Njalsson, you earlier testified that you had been retained by Dr. Haverly on the matter of the patent application for a new spell that he was developing. Is that correct?" Greenwood began.

"Yes it is."

"And how long had you been retained by him in that capacity?"

"I believe that he first approached me in early March. We signed an agreement formalizing the arrangement on March 12th."

"So by the time of the events of June 13 you had been working for Dr. Haverly for three months?"

"That is correct."

"And as part of your work you were privy to certain aspects of his work as part of the patent application?"

"Yes. Any patent application has to include information on prior art, on how the device or process the patent is to cover is novel, and similar matters. I had obtained from Dr.

Haverly a detailed description of the spell with the omission of a few key details which he wished to keep to himself as long as possible."

"But still, the information you had in your possession was potentially quite valuable, was it not?"

"Yes. It amounted to the fruits of several years research on the part of Dr. Haverly."

"Was Dr. Haverly at all concerned with the security of the material in you possession?"

"Yes, quite naturally. I went over the security measures in my office with him in detail. As I remember, he was quite impressed. I believe that is one of the reasons he chose to retain me instead of a more established firm."

"So these security measures of yours are unusual?"

"I would like to think so. I developed most of them myself."

"Ah, yes. As you are a wizard in addition to an attorney. I take it the security measures you are referring to are magical in nature."

"Yes."

"Would you care to describe them to the court?"

"I would prefer not to. Part of the effectiveness of any security arrangement is the fact that its nature is not known to those who would try to breech it."

"I understand, Mr. Njalsson. The details are unimportant for our purposes and can remain your secret. But I would like to know if there had been any attempt to breech your security."

"There were."

"In the period between March 12 and June 13?"

"Yes. On three occasions."

"Could you describe those attempts?"

"The first occurred on March 19. The lock on my door, a conventional, non-magical one was picked. However, because of certain wards guarding the premises, they were unable to enter the office proper. I have to assume that they were not wizards. A second attempt was made on April 20. This time they were able to enter my office. Some papers that were on my desk were gone through, but as far as I could tell, nothing was taken. I keep any sensitive documents in a special safe which was not touched."

"Do you have any idea what the thieves were looking for?"

"No. It is in the nature of my practice that at any one time I may have valuable or sensitive information from a number of clients. However, at that time, I did have the documentation provided by Dr. Haverly in my possession."

"Did you report either of these occurrences to the police, Mr. Njalsson?"

"No, I did not."

"May I ask why?"

"The first attempt had ended in complete failure. I didn't see the point. The second attempt was more serious, but not successful. Frankly, I didn't think that the police would be of much use and I wanted to avoid the publicity. The idea that my office was the target of thieves might dissuade future clients."

"I understand. You said there were three occurrences."

"Yes. This was on June 11. Again, the thieves succeeded in getting through the door. They also discovered the presence of my safe which had remained concealed in the two earlier break-ins. They tried to force their way into it using some rather potent means of a magical nature."

"I take it that they did not succeed?"

"No. Fortunately, I returned to my office and they were interrupted and forced to flee."

"Were you concerned?"

"Of course. I took several additional steps to secure the premises."

"Did you inform any of your clients of these break-ins?"

"After the last one, I contacted Dr. Haverly as his documentation was clearly the most valuable item in my office at the time. He informed me that he, too, had experienced several attempts to break into his laboratory. I suggested that it might be wise if I reviewed the state of his measures and he agreed. That resulted in the appointment for June 13."

"Now, Mr. Njalsson, do you have any idea who was behind the attempted break-ins at either your office or Dr. Haverly's laboratory?"

"Nothing concrete, nothing that could be acted on. Both Dr. Haverly and myself had our suspicions. As I said earlier, word of the nature of Dr. Haverly's work had leaked out. He had been approached by several parties who claimed that they were interested in investing in his spell. Dr. Haverly chose to decline the offers, but one of the parties, Alan Rigsby, was persistent. I believe there were threats implied at one point."

"What was the nature of these threats?"

"The party who made them was very careful in his wording, but according to Dr. Haverly he felt his life might be in danger."

"And were you ever approached by this party in regards to Dr. Haverly's process?"

"Yes. One night as I was walking to my car I was approached by a man who said he would 'make it worth my while' if I allowed him access to the documentation Dr, Haverly had left with me. I declined. He seemed about to get unpleasant when a police patrol car drove past. I knew the officer inside and waved to him. When I looked around, the man who had approached me was gone. Later, when I compared notes with Dr. Haverly, we agreed that it might well be the same man as had threatened him."

"Did you know the identity of this man?"

"Not at that time. Later, after June 13, I realized that it was Alan Rigsby."

"I see. Now what was Dr. Haverly's response to these threats?"

"He told me that he felt he could deal with them."

"And what did you take him to mean by that, Mr. Njalsson?"

"I took it to mean that he felt that his security measures were adequate. He is a very talented wizard. And, as I have stated earlier, he had agreed to a review of these measures by Mr. Schmidts and myself."

"You did not take it to mean that he would take direct action against this Alan Rigsby?"

"No, I did not."

"Did he make mention of having an appointment with Alan Rigsby the night of June 13th?"

"No, he did not. As I have stated, he had arranged to meet with me and Mr. Schmidts that night."

"I see," Greenwood responded, seeming to weigh the words carefully. "Earlier, the medical examiner testified that on your suggestion he had reexamined the remains of Alan Rigsby, specifically his feet. Are you aware of what he found?"

"Yes. He found that Rigsby's left foot was cloven."

"And did you have reason to believe that that was what he might find?"

"I did. The nature of Dr. Haverly's defenses on the night of June 13 led me to suspect that Rigsby might not be human. That, and the fact that his defenses, in the form of a pentagram, were successful."

"And what, exactly, is the significance of Dr. Manly's discovery?"

"Objection.   The defense is asking for the witnesses opinion."

"Your Honor.   I would remind the court that Mr. Njalsson not only has a degree in metaphysics from one of the most prestigious institutions of higher learning in this country, but is also a holder of a First Class Magician's license.   As such, I believe he should be considered an expert witness."

"Overruled, Mr. Cline," Judge Wilson pronounced. "The witness may answer the question."

"When a demon takes on human form, the transformation is never complete.   Some part always remains unchanged to betray the demonic nature.   The most common indication is a cloven foot."

"Just such a foot as it appears Mr. Rigby possessed?"

"Exactly."

"Now, to return to the events of June 13, your associate, Mr. Schmidts, has testified that he sensed a spell which he said emanated from a dark force.   Do you concur with his assessment."

"Mr. Schmidts is much more sensitive to such forces than I am.   However, I did detect the presence of Black Magic."

"And that could not have been due to any spell of Dr. Haverly's?"

"The pentagram, while unusual in its execution, was clearly a form of White or protective magic.   The transmutation spell, of which I have some detailed knowledge through my work on the patent application, was an example of what is now coming to be known as Green or natural magic.   There was nothing amongst the materials that Dr. Haverly had on hand to indicate that he had employed any spell involving Black Magic."

"Yet the presence of such magic was detectable in the room on that night."

"In my opinion, yes."

"And what do you think the purpose of that spell might have been?"

"It clearly had been directed at breaking through the protection offered by the pentagram Dr. Haverly had drawn on the floor of his laboratory."

"And what would have been the results if that protection had failed?"

"Without knowing the exact nature of the spell, it is hard to say, but quite possibly it might have resulted in the destruction of anything and anyone within the pentagram."

"In other words, Dr. Haverly might well have inferred that his life was in danger?"

"That would have been a reasonable assumption. It's the one I would have made."

"Thank you. No further questions."

"Mr. Cline," the judge said. "It seems only fair to grant you an opportunity to cross examine the witness."

"Thank you, your Honor."

"Mr. Njalsson. You have referred to the pentagram drawn by Dr. Haverly. In your earlier testimony you said that it would have taken him several minutes at least to draw such a figure. Is that correct?"

"At least. Quite possibly longer. It was quite an elaborate figure and I haven't had an opportunity to see Dr. Haverly at work."

"And, as I understand it, such a figure can actually be drawn quite a bit ahead of time and then activated at the last moment by sealing it with a—I believe you called it a 'sigil'. Is that correct."

"Yes, that is correct."

"So, is it possible that Dr. Haverly drew this pentagram at some earlier time knowing that he would be meeting Mr. Rigsby that night?"

"Quite possible."

"And that he did so with the express purpose of confronting and killing Mr. Rigsby."

"The pentagram would only offer protection. It was not an offensive spell. Its purpose was to prevent anyone from coming in contact with Dr. Haverly. It could not, in and of itself injure anyone or anything unless they tried to breech that protection."

"But, could Dr. Haverly not have planned to cast his spell of transmutation from within the protection of the pentagram?"

"Objection. The prosecution is asking the witness to make a conjecture about possibilities."

"Overruled. However, I would remind the jury that we are talking about the possibility of something occurring, not the fact that it actually did occur. Please answer the question, Mr. Njalsson."

"It is possible, but I would have thought it a very risky proposition. A pentagram acts much like a two way street limiting the actions of those inside as well as outside. To cast such a spell as Dr. Haverly's transmutation spell from inside that pentagram was an act of desperation. The amount of energy required would have been enormous and the toll it took on the caster could well have proved fatal. I saw no signs that Dr. Haverly had in any way planned to cast such a spell before he drew the pentagram."

The prosecutor stood for a moment as if thinking what to ask next, then with a shrug said, "No further questions, your honor."

☆   ☆   ☆   ☆   ☆

"The prosecution may now make it's summation," the judge stated from his place on the bench.

Cline rose from his seat behind the prosecutor's table. For a moment he stood with his hands on his lapels staring at Dr. Haverly behind the defense's table, then he strode to a position before the box where the jury was seated.

"Ladies and gentlemen of the jury, I think that the prosecution has proved beyond any doubt that the defendant, Dr. Haverly, did on the night of 13 June of this year, through means of a powerful magical spell, kill Alan Rigsby by transmuting all of the carbon in his body into silicon, in effect, turning a living, breathing being into a pillar of sand. We have as facts that Dr. Haverly is an expert in such transformations and that the 'statue' found in Dr. Haverly's laboratory is clearly not a statue at all, but a human body which has undergone the transmutation described. You will note that the defense has not contested this assertion.

"It is the contention of the prosecution that Dr. Haverly, whether he felt threatened for some reason or whether he was just concerned with protecting the secrets of his new process, did arrange to lure Alan Rigsby into his laboratory. That in this laboratory he had protected himself with an elaborate pentagram, a device that would have taken some time and planning to produce, and which it is unlikely that he would have had time to draw in response to the sudden appearance of Alan Rigsby. And that when Alan Rigsby showed up in his laboratory, he worked this spell of magic and so did take away the life of that individual.

"At no point has the defense disputed the essentials of this sequence of events. In fact, I believe that the sole argument of the defense is that Dr. Haverly felt so threatened by Mr. Rigsby that he acted in self defense.

"I will have the jury note that at no time did Dr. Haverly contact the police or any other authority about a perceived threat. Is this the act of an innocent man? Instead, we have had a witness state that Dr. Haverly had assured him that 'he could handle things on his own.' This, to me, ladies and gentlemen, sounds like a man who had decided to take a very clear and premeditated action. That, I think, is the point which you must decide. Did Dr. Haverly act out of self defense, feeling that he had no other recourse, or was his plan from the beginning to lure Alan Rigsby to his death.

"If it is the latter, then you, the jury, must find Dr. Haverly guilty of murder in the first degree by the use of magic. I know that this is a most serious charge, but I think it is the most reasonable, the only, conclusion that can be drawn from the evidence as it has been presented at this trial."

With that, Cline sat down. From the expression on his face it was clear that he was less than sure that he had convinced the jury of his case, indeed that he had a case. But at least he had done his job.

It was now time for the defense's closing statement. Unlike his opponent, Walter Greenwood was the picture of confidence as he paused facing the jury before making his final presentation.

"Ladies and gentlemen of the jury," he began. His tone was not that of an orator, but of someone engaged in conversation. This, of course, was the secret of Greenwood's success, his ability to connect with a jury not as an attorney, but as a peer, even as a friend.

"We, that is my client and I, do not dispute the fact that Dr. Haverly did work a spell that transmuted Alan Rigsby into a pillar of silicon. It would be foolish of us to do so. After all, that is what actually happened. All the efforts of the prosecution to dwell on this point are irrelevant. We acknowledge that Dr. Haverly is a world renowned expert in the subject of transmutation. We acknowledge that the silicon 'statue' found in his laboratory is in fact the remains of Alan Rigsby. We acknowledge that his current state is due to a spell worked by my client. We have never, in the course of this trial, denied any of this."

Here, the council for the defense paused for a moment. Egil, from his place in the gallery could see that the eyes of each of the jurors was focused on Greenwood's face.

"The real issues for you to decide, members of the jury,—and there are in fact two of them—are these, One, did Dr. Haverly act in a manner consistent with self-defense as defined by the laws of this state. If so, then you must find him not guilty on that basis. The second point, which the prosecution has chosen to ignore, is whether Alan Rigsby was in fact human." Greenwood paused for a second, then continued, "whether he was human or a demon. If you decide that there are reasonable grounds for the latter being the case, then you must again find my client not guilty. The laws of state are quite clear on this point, murder, in whatever degree, is defined as the willful causing of the death of a human being. Not a plant, not an animal, and certainly not a demon. Only a human being.

"Of course," Greenwood said with a smile, "if you decide that Dr. Haverly acted in self-defense against a demon, then you must rule him not-guilty. This is not one of those cases where a double negative yields a positive." The jury seemed to appreciate Greenwood's little joke.

"Now the law is quite clear on the matter of self-defense. To invoke it there are two requirements. One, the accused must have reasonable grounds for feeling that his life is threatened. Two, he must have taken reasonable measures to avoid a confrontation if those are available to him."

"Now as to the first point, you have heard the testimony of Mr. Njalsson about how he had been threatened, about how several attempts had been made to break into his office in connection with documents that he was holding for Dr. Haverly, and how Alan Rigsby seemed to be the person behind these actions. I will point out, that this does not have to be proved, only that a reasonable person, such as a member of this jury, might infer that this was the case. You have also heard testimony to the effect that Dr. Haverly had also received threats from Rigsby. Dr. Haverly, as is his right, has chosen not to testify in his own defense. However, we do have direct evidence, again from Mr. Njalsson that Dr. Haverly was concerned about the security arrangements at his laboratory.

"Now the prosecution has contended that Dr. Haverly lured Alan Rigsby to his laboratory with the express purpose of murdering him. That Dr. Haverly prepared in advance an elaborate pentagram from in which he could work his spell of transmutation from a position of relative safety. And that when Alan Rigsby showed up at the laboratory, Dr. Haverly killed him, as he had planned, with a transmutation spell.

"I contend. Well I contend, ladies and gentlemen, that that just doesn't make sense. Why would he chose to lure Rigsby to his laboratory for purposes of murder at the same time that he had made an appointment with Mr. Njalsson, the one person most likely to grasp what he had done? In my experience, one doesn't usually invite witnesses to a murder."

"Now, if one grants that the rather unusual choice of a transmutation spell was a murder weapon, why wait behind a rather defensive barricade, allow the murder victim ample time to unleash his own magical weaponry before invoking this spell, when the accused could just as easily worked the spell the moment the victim walked through the door, or was walking up the path to the laboratory, or was getting out of his car? Now everyone seems to agree that Dr. Haverly is a pretty smart fellow. Why, then, would he chose to act in such a stupid way?

"Isn't it much more likely that Dr. Haverly, waiting in his laboratory for Mr. Njalsson and his colleague, sensed the approach of Alan Rigsby; that fearing for his life and suspecting the demonic nature of Rigsby, he hastily drew a protective pentagram, and then finding himself under magical assault by powerful black forces as a last resort chose to work the spell of transmutation; a spell that nearly took his own life as well as that of Rigsby? Isn't this the more reasonable conclusion to draw?"

Greenwood paused a moment to catch his breath as did the members of the jury. In a softer voice he continued, "As to the second issue, that of the question of Alan Rigsby's humanity, you have heard in the report of the medical examiner of the anatomical anomaly of the left foot. You have heard the explanation of Mr. Njalsson as to this being the mark of the demon. You have also heard from both Mr. Njalsson and Mr. Schmidts how they sensed the presence of powerful black magics in the laboratory of Dr. Haverly, magics, that these two learned practitioners assured us were not the work of Dr. Haverly. It is up to you, the members of the jury, to decide if Alan Rigsby was in fact a demon. But if you so decide, than you must on that basis declare my client innocent of the charge of murder.

"Now ladies and gentlemen, the charge of first degree murder, especially first degree murder by means of magic, is a most serious charge. The law states that to convict my client of this most serious crime you must be sure beyond a reasonable shadow of a doubt that Dr. Haverly did not act in self defense and that Alan Rigsby was not a demon. If you are not sure of either of these points beyond that shadow of a doubt, then you must rule that my client is not guilty of the crime of which he is accused.

"The state has placed a great deal of trust in you, ladies and gentlemen of the jury, in the faith that you will act to the best of your abilities to weigh the evidence presented to you and make a fair and unbiased decision on that evidence and the requirements of the law. My client and I also place are faith and trust in you. Thank you."

Greenwood sat down next to his client, with no look of victory or defeat upon his face, only an expression of weariness.

The judge gave his final instructions to the jury who were then ushered out for their deliberation. It was a little over an hour before they filed back in and took their place in the jury box.

"Ladies and gentlemen of the jury," the judge addressed them, "have you reached a verdict?"

The foreman of the jury rose and in a clear voice she stated, "We have, your honor."

"And what is that verdict?"

"We find the defendant not guilty of the charge of first degree murder."

RAY-GUNS ON STAR CITY BY GREG FOWLKES

A PREVIEW OF A SHORT STORY FROM THE UPCOMING BOOK - *STAR CITY STORIES*

Ray-Guns on Star City

The Blue Moon was different than other bars on Star City. It was dark and cool. But mostly it was quiet. There wasn't any sound projector blaring the latest jive samba. There weren't any holocasters spewing pitches for products no one needed. There wasn't even a televisor showing sporting events except for during the Worlds Series. That's one of the reasons I liked the place.

Mostly though, I go there because it's across the street from where I live, a not too crummy apartment building on the fringes of New Minglewood. New Minglewood is the district of Star City where the grifters, whores and all the other low-lifes with no regular employment live. They live there because the rent is cheap. Also it's the only place that will have them.

Star City was built on a hunk of rock that failed as a planet. Once a fortnight it orbits around a star that never made it to the big time, but is doomed to spend eternity as a brown dwarf stuck in the middle of nowhere. There's no reason at all for Star City to exist except that it happens to be at the place where a half dozen space routes intersect making it a convenient place for transshipments and for making connections. When they discovered it, they hollowed it out, spun it up to give it the semblance of gravity it could never generate on its own, and built a pair of docking rings at each end. They can handle a hundred ships at a time, and there are always a dozen more parked in orbit waiting a berth.

Half the commerce of human space passes through Star City, and with it comes half the population, or at least so it seems. Star City has grown up catering to the needs and whims of those travelers making a layover whether they are moguls or deck hands. You can buy any sort of food or beverage known. You can find entertainment to pass the time until your ship leaves. You can gamble a fortune away at a dozen casinos; or bet your last dollar.

Me, I was nursing a whiskey and soda in the middle of the afternoon. I knew it was whiskey because it was brown and ninety proof. If it had been clear it would have been gin or vodka. In either case, it had never been within a light year of Scotland or Tennessee or any other place on any respectable planet circling a real sun. I was drinking in the middle of the afternoon because I didn't have anything better to do.

I was alone in the place except for the bartender and one other customer who sat at the far end with a stack of Crockett dollars piled up on the bar in front of him. Every fifteen minutes the barkeep would bring him a shot of something blue and remove two dollar coins from the pile. He never seemed to take the empty glasses away. There looked to be about a dozen.

The guy was nondescript looking, about middle age, middle height, middle weight. He looked like he might be a travelling salesman. There was something that looked like it might be a sample case resting on the floor next to his barstool. He was leaning on the bar staring into space. In that position it was hard to tell if he was drunk or just weary of the world. He'd looked up for a minute when I had walked in, but after giving me the once-over returned to contemplating the blue liquid in the shot glass in front of him.

The bartender knew me well enough to know that I wasn't interested in conversation. The salesman wasn't talking, either. That suited the bartender just fine as it gave him plenty of time to polish glasses with the dirty rag he kept tucked in his belt.

It was almost with annoyance that he looked up when the door opened to accept a new denizen of the bar. This guy was anything but ordinary. Just shy of two meters tall he was wearing a flash suit that looked as if it cost what the average Joe made in a month. He had what is euphemistically called a "spacer tan." Of course, real spacers never see the light of a sun and are normally pale as ghosts. I was thinking he was in the wrong bar in the wrong part of Star City.

He walked up to the bar and motioned for the bartender. Like he needed to attract attention when there were only two other customers in the place.

"I'm looking for a woman. Tall, good-looking, red hair. She's wearing a black dress cinched at the waist and black, high-heeled boots. Has she been in here?"

"Sorry mister," the bartender said. "There ain't been no woman looking like that in here all day, and my shift started at eight." Truth was there hadn't been any woman in there all day, and certainly not one like he had described.

"You sure? She said she'd meet me here."

"Nope. No one like that in here today. You want a drink while you wait?"

"No, I'll pass. Are there any other bars named the Blue Moon on Star City?"

"Not that I know of. There is a Red Planet Saloon down by the spacedocks, but I wouldn't go there. It's a dive from what I hear." I knew the place. The bartender was right. The Red Planet was definitely not a place to go looking for a good-looking red head. Or for anything else unless it was trouble.

"Thanks. If she comes in here, tell her I was here."

"Who shall I say?"

"She'll know who."

He turned and headed for the door. The guy at the other end of the bar stood up, his hand reaching inside his jacket. For a wonder he didn't fall down. He called out, "Yano!"

The guy at the door turned to face him, a look of concern on his face. There were what sounded like three soft sneezes and suddenly three red spots appeared on his chest just where his heart would be. He looked for a moment stunned and then he slumped to the floor.

I looked towards the guy at the end of the bar. He was holding a needle gun in his right hand. It was an assassin's weapon, small and quiet, firing tiny darts at hypersonic speeds. I knew then that he was no salesman.

I raised my hands to show I was unarmed. Frankly, I didn't think there was a chance in hell of my getting out of their alive, but even if I had been packing heat I knew I couldn't beat him. Not if he could place three darts within a circle smaller than a fist at ten meters in a dimly lit bar. The barkeep took his clue from me and raised his hands as well, the look of fear on his face.

The salesman/assassin scooped up the pile of Crockett dollars from the bar leaving two as a tip. That gave me some hope unless he had a twisted sense of humor. He stuffed the coins in his jacket pocket, then picked up his case with the same hand. All this time he was holding the needle gun in his right pointed nowhere in particular. He strode nonchalantly towards the door, stepping around the body. As he reached the door the needle gun disappeared into his jacket. Then he was gone.

"Holy Shiva! Mathew, Mark, George, and Ringo! What do we do now?"

The barkeep's theology might be confused, but I shared his sentiment.

"I suggest we wait ten minutes, then you call the cops," I said, trying to sound calm and like I knew what I was doing. I wasn't either.

"You going to be here then?" he asked.

"No reason not to. I still got some of my drink left."

I waited five and then poked my nose out the door, looking both ways up and down the street. There was no sign of an assassin with a sample case. No red head in a black dress either. I ducked back into the bar.

"You might as well call the cops, now," I said, resuming my place at the bar.

The cops showed up in ten, a couple of plain-clothes men. I knew one of them slightly, a big, beefy detective sergeant named Latimer. He knew me, too. Star City cops aren't particularly bright or honest, but they make up for it with attitude.

"Well if it ain't Frank Sladek, the private dick. Did you have to off one of your clients?"

"Not me, Latimer. I was just in here having a quiet drink." I gave him a brief synopsis of the events. He looked skeptical. I couldn't blame him.

"You packing, Sladek?"

"Not me. You know I hate to carry a weapon if I don't have to. Those things are hazardous to your health."

"Always the funny guy, Sladek. Well, if you ain't packing, you won't mind if Rosseti here pats you down."

"I've got no objection as long as he doesn't get fresh."

Rosseti gave me a dirty look. The pat down was efficient and more thorough than it needed to be. "He's clean."

"So what were you doing here, Sladek? And don't give me a line about you just came in for a drink."

"It's true. I live in the apartments just across the street. Business has been slow. I felt the need for human companionship."

"In a bar empty of customers?" Latimer asked.

"I just wanted a quiet drink."

"Well you got it, didn't you?" he remarked sardonically.

"It was quiet most of the time."

"So you want me to believe that this guy walks in and asks for a red-headed broad, this other guy shouts out 'Yano', pops three needles into his chest and walks out leaving you and the barkeep still breathing?"

"That's about the size of it, sergeant. No one is more surprised than me that I'm still standing."

"That's Detective Sergeant. And your story stinks, Sladek," Latimer responded.

"I can't help it. Ask the bartender."

Latimer went over the same ground with the bartender and got the same story. That seemed to annoy him. The fact that he was beginning to think it was the truth didn't help matters any. Meanwhile, Rosseti had been poking his nose into all the corners coming up with nothing.

The doctor from the Medical Examiner's office came while Latimer was still questioning the bartender. He was a blueskin from Asimov III. The high oxygen content of his home world had resulted in an adaptation which gave a pale blue cast to his skin in the relatively lower oxygen ratio of Star City which was roughly that of Earth. I noticed the small oxygen bottle clipped to his waist that allowed him to breathe a shot whenever he felt hypoxia setting in. I wondered what he had done to get himself exiled to Star City.

He did his thing, taking holograms of the body, measuring body temperature, taking a blood sample, doing a scan of the wound.

"Well, doc?"

"He's dead, Latimer."

"I know that. What was the cause of death?"

"Three flechettes from a needle gun to the heart."

"Poisoned?"

"Not that I can tell. No toxins in his blood at least. All three darts penetrated the heart causing massive blood loss. He died almost immediately."

"Awful good shooting, wasn't it?" Latimer commented.

"Yes it was, wasn't it," the doc agreed.

"Can you tell me how far the shooter was from the victim?"

"Not exactly. It wasn't close range. More like five to ten meters. Like you said, good shooting. Well, if you've no further need for the body, I'll take it off your hands."

"Cart him away, doc. I ain't got no use for it."

The doctor wheeled the body out to the meat wagon that was waiting outside in the street.

"You done with me, Latimer?" I asked.

"Your current residence on file?"

"Yeah. Right across the street. Number 44."

"OK. You can go. But don't leave town." We both got a chuckle out of that.

THE FICTIONAL DETECTIVE SPEAKS WITH THE DEAD
BY GREG FOWLKES

Sneak Preview!

THE FICTIONAL DETECTIVE SPEAKS WITH THE DEAD

I was sitting in my office going through my files. This was a couple of weeks after I'd solved the Handler murder. That case had left me with a lot of unanswered questions about the nature of reality and I'd gone into a kind of funk that ended up in a week long drunk. After I'd sobered up I came to the conclusion that no matter what the truth was, there was nothing I could do about it and I might as well just get on with life. After all, it wasn't shaping up as such a bad life. Janet and I were talking about getting married. Janet is the kind of dame men dream about, a tall, good looking with curves in all the right places. She was smart and had money, too. We'd be fixed for life with what Handler had left her in his will.

I was thinking about getting out of the business, and was trying to tie up loose ends. I wasn't really looking for any new cases, but I was still listed in the phone book and business directory and it still said "Private Detective" under my name on the frosted glass in the office door. I wasn't completely surprised then, when there came a tentative knock on that door. It was a woman's knock, quick, light, not so much demanding attention as imploring for it.

I stood up, stashed the bottle of bourbon and the glass in the bottom drawer and went to open the door. The last time I had done that, the woman had been Janet, a leggy blonde with looks straight out of a fashion magazine. My visitor was nothing like that.

She was a big woman, not fat, but ample, probably in her mid fifties. She was dressed expensively in a dress and coat that actually fit her and made her seem thinner than she really was. Her hair had been styled recently in one of those cuts that women who can afford it wear. She reminded me as much as anything of the heavy set broad who always played the older rich dame in the Marx brothers movies. You know the one I mean, the one who never seemed to get the jokes.

"Mr. Slade?" she asked tentatively.

"That's me. What can I do for you?"

"I believe you are a—a private detective?"

"That's what it says on the door, though I'm thinking of getting out of the racket."

"Oh--, I'm sorry. I thought--." I could see she had trouble on her mind. I never could turn down a dame in trouble, even an older one.

"Please, come in. The least I can do is hear your story. After all, you came all this way down here to talk to me."

"That's very kind, Mr. Slade." She entered the office and took the chair facing the desk. Despite her size she moved with a certain kind of grace. I shut the office door and sat in my desk chair.

When I was seated she said, "I don't quite know where to start."

"Why don't we start with the simple things. Like your name."

"Yes. Of course. I'm Geraldine Duville. My husband was Herbert Duville. He ran a trucking business, Tri-State Transportation Services, until he died recently."

"My condolences, Mrs. DuVille. Just what did you want to consult with me about?"

"Well, it's like this, Mr. Slade. Some time before his death, my husband took on some partners. He needed some capital to expand the business."

"How was the business doing, if you don't mind my asking?"

"Quite well, I think. I never bothered too much about the business. I left that to Herbert. But we had always lived quite comfortably. Herbert was a good provider." I could hear the love in her voice. "I'm not sure why Herbert felt the need to expand, but he seemed to think it was important."

"And these partners he brought on? Were they on the up and up?"

"They seemed to be at first. They were just going to invest some money and leave the running of the business to my husband. But after awhile they wanted to become more involved. He never said anything about it, but I could tell that Herbert wasn't altogether happy with the situation."

"Any particulars?"

"As I said, Mr. Slade, I never involved myself with the business. And then Herbert died, and that changed everything."

"Just how did he die?"

"An accident, or so I thought—"

"But something has caused you to change your mind?"

"I'm getting to that. The arrangement as I understand it was that my husband retained 51% of the company while Mr. McClure and Mr. Trentino split the remainder of the shares between them. However, there appears to have been an unfortunate clause placed in the contract by which they invested. In the event of the death of any of the partners, their share of the company would be split between the surviving partners. The result was that when my husband died his share of the company went to Mr. McClure and Mr. Trentino, and I was left with nothing."

"Your husband didn't leave anything to you?"

"Oh, no, Mr. Slade. I don't want you to think that. He left me the house, of course and some investments. There was also a large insurance policy that he had taken out shortly after we were married. I don't want you to think that he left me a pauper. I may not be able to live quite as well as before, but I shall get by. But it's the thought of the company that Herbert worked so hard to build just going to those-- others that bothers me."

"You've talked to a lawyer about this, haven't you?"

"Yes. He said that it was an unusual agreement, but it seemed perfectly legal. He didn't hold out much hope for litigation, I'm afraid."

"I'm sorry about your troubles, Mrs. Duville, but I'm not quite sure what it is you want me to do?"

"What I want you to do, Mr. Slade is come to a séance."

"A séance?" I said with surprise. It was about the last thing I had expected.

"Yes, a séance, Mr. Slade. I know that this may sound to you like a strange request, but I have been in touch with my husband, and he wishes to speak with you personally. There is something that he wants to tell you."

"You've talked to your husband? At a séance?"

"Yes."

"And he asked for me?" I couldn't keep the skepticism out of my voice.

"Yes. He was quite particular about that point. At the last session he asked for you. That's why I came down here, Mr. Slade. I assure you that I don't normally employ private detectives."

"I didn't think you did, Mrs. Duville. I admit that I have very little experience with these kind of things, but isn't this an awfully specific request for someone who is dead to communicate."

"I assure you, Mr. Slade, that this séance was not a silly parlor game like those Ouija boards. The Professor is a very serious person."

"The professor?"

"Yes, the medium. Professor Longwell. He's quite well known, Mr. Slade."

"I'm sure he is." Probably by half the bunko squads in the state, I thought to myself.

"I detect a note of doubt, Mr. Slade, but I am willing to pay you for your time, whatever your standard rate is. Please, won't you come? I'm a desperate woman." She seemed on the point of tears.

"It's a hundred dollars a day. Plus expenses."

"What's a hundred dollars."

"That's my standard fee, Mrs. Duville. When is this séance?"

"Tonight, if you can make it. I'm sure I can arrange it with the Professor. He's been so helpful."

"I'm sure he has. As it is, I am available tonight. What time?"

"Would nine o'clock be possible."

"That shouldn't be a problem." Janet was going to fix me dinner, but we'd be done in plenty of time.

"Fine. Here's the address," she handed me a card with her name and address.

"Tonight, then. And don't worry, you can pay me after the séance."

"Thank you, Mr. Slade. I'll be waiting for you."

She rose and I escorted her to the door.

After she left, I thought about the deal. Was she just some poor widow being preyed upon by a charlatan? Or was there more to this séance business? I didn't really believe in ghosts. On the other hand, I didn't not believe in them either. I'd seen enough strange things lately to keep an open mind. Of anyone in the world, I was the last to question the reality of such things.   Or the reality of anything, for that matter.

FROM THE WIZARD AT LAW SERIES BY GREG FOWLKES

THE LAWS OF MAGIC

Egil Njalsson was an aspiring lawyer. A lawyer with a difference. Not only had he passed the bar, but he had an undergraduate degree from the most prestigious school of magic in the country, the California Institute of Thaumaturgy. Needless to say his caseload and clients tended to the unusual. Like witches; or vampires. And the opposition, well they were likely to be demons. But Egil Njalsson had sworn an oath to uphold the law of the land, and... *The Laws of Magic*!

TRIAL BY MAGIC

Egil Njalsson is just another practicing attorney. Except, that is, for the occasional unusual client. Such as the ghost who retained his services using e-mail. Or the wolf who has been cursed by an Indian shaman to turn into a human during the full moon. Or the Leprechaun who is facing the loss of his saloon. Even when the clients are human, they have unusual problems like the Creole chef accused of making a rival a zombie or the scientist accused of transmuting a man into a statue of silicon. Yet somehow, Egil manages to resolve all his client's problems whether legal or magical. Of course it helps that he is a wizard as well as a lawyer.

Trial by Magic includes five new tales from the same world as *The Laws of Magic*.

FROM THE MURDER ON MARS SERIES BY GREG FOWLKES

BLOOD REDS SANDS OF MARS

On Mars the wind was rising. The grains of sand could be heard abrading the thin aluminum skin that was the only protection against the outside. On the far side of Olympus Mons a prospector lies dead in the sand. Inspector Erik McKernan, head of the handful of men that make up the small Martian police force must find the killer while threading the maze of corporate and international politics that govern the planet, and he must do it while trying to survive . . .The Blood Red Sands of Mars!

A DEATH AT STATION ALPHA

Station Alpha, a remote Martian research facility isolated by a planet wide dust storm. When one of the scientists is found murdered, it falls to Inspector McKernan to determine which of the remaining twelve people at the station wielded the fatal weapon. But, as the crime was committed in a locked laboratory with no possible access and all the suspects would seem to have unbreakable alibis, it will take all his skills as a detective to solve the puzzle of A Death at Station Alpha. Thirty years in the making, the long awaited sequel to The Blood Red Sands of Mars.

A Corpse in Hut Town

Hut Town is the remnants of the original Martian settlement; a collection of inflatable buildings abandoned by the Trust Authority and the mining corporations and now occupied by those catering to the baser needs of miners and construction workers in for a spree. But when a corpse is found in one of the service tunnels, Chief Inspector McKernan is called in.

He has plenty of questions. Who's body is it? How did they die? How did they get to Mars in the first place, and why weren't they missed? And the most important one on the Inspector's mind— are there any more bodies down there?

Murder at the Mars Club

The Mars Club was the sanctuary of the rich and powerful on Mars, so when one of the members is found dead, Chief Inspector is called in to solve the case as discretely as possible. Will the solution of the case prove to be the one man he'd least like to implicate?

FROM THE FICTIONAL DETECTIVE SERIES BY GREG FOWLKES

THE FICTIONAL DETECTIVE

Mystery writer Ezekial O. Handler has been killed in a suspicious car crash. Private detective Frank Slade has been hired by Handler's beautiful girlfriend to investigate. Handler, seemingly with a premonition of his death, has left a trail of clues. Can Slade discover the murderer, or will he instead uncover a secret that will shake his existence to the core?

A FICTIONAL DETECTIVE TRIFECTA

The Fictional Detective has gotten out of the Private Investigator game. Instead, he's trying to write hard-boiled masterpieces such as *Death Buys a Condo*. But despite the fact that the door of his office now says WRITER, some of his clients haven't gotten the word. And a strange lot of clients they are. A man that only contacts him during séances because, well, he's dead; a female impersonator who has inherited a house that's just a little too haunted for the market, and a small time gambler who's trying to end an affair with Lady Luck.

Three All New Novellas featuring the Fictional Detective!

SPACE OPERA NOIR!

STAR CITY STORIES: A COLLECTION OF STORIES FEATURING FRANK SLADEK
BY GREG FOWLKES

The mean streets of Star City, a hollowed out asteroid circling a failed star in the middle of nowhere breed a special sort of man. With grifters, hoodlums, and two-bit con-men from every planet In human space trying to make the big score, it takes someone like Frank Sladek, sometime private detective, sometime finder of lost items, to navigate the maze of corruption and double-crosses that is Star City. As quick with his wit as with a needler or laser pistol, Sladek can handle anyone, except maybe the dames. These are just a few of the Star City Stories.

BOOKS BY GREG FOWLKES

From the Wizard at Law Series:
The Laws of Magic
Trial by Magic

From the Murder on Mars Series:
Blood Red Sands of Mars
A Death at Station Alpha
A Corpse in Hut Town
Murder at the Mars Club

From the Fictional Detective Series:
The Fictional Detective
A Fictional Detective Trifecta

Star City Stories: A Collection of Stories Featuring Frank Sladek

The Uncorrupted Corpse

Tequila Visions

Cargo From Paradise

Ice Viking

The Fictional Press
www.TheFictionalPress.com

The Fictional Press is an imprint of Intrepid Ink, LLC. Find out more at www.TheFictionalPress.com.

About Intrepid Ink, LLC

Intrepid Ink, LLC provides full publishing services to authors of fiction and non-fiction books, eBooks and websites. From editing to formatting, from publishing to marketing, Intrepid Ink gets your creative works into the hands of the people who want to read them. Find out more at www.IntrepidInk.com.